CW00518923

C.S. Guild

Minnie

C.S. Guild

Minnie

1st Edition | ISBN: 978-3-75238-317-1

Place of Publication: Frankfurt am Main, Germany

Year of Publication: 2020

Outlook Verlag GmbH, Germany.

Reproduction of the original.

MINNIE

BY THE AUTHOR OF "VIOLET."

CHAPTER I.

RODOCANACHI.

Somewhere in Massachusetts is a little town as beautiful as a garden. Nay, in summer-time I think this place is prettier than a garden; for it is not laid out in long, stiff beds and paths; but the roads wind about like rivers under its shady trees, and, wherever you see a bed of flowers, a cosey little house is sure to rise up in its midst; and then the hills,—Did you ever read about the giant, who wouldn't give the fairies any peace, but chopped them up for mince-meat, and did all kinds of wicked things, till they resolved to kill him, if they could?

The fairy queen, who was very wise, knew that the giant's strength lay in a great brass helmet which he wore; so she told her people to watch, and, if ever he laid it aside, to steal this, and hide it away.

Now, one summer's day, the giant went hunting, and had such good success that he came home with his arms full of game, tired and warm enough.

I don't remember the giant's name: perhaps it was Ugolino, or Loeschigk, or Rodocanachi. We'll call it Rodocanachi. Down he threw his game,—the deer and squirrels he had killed to eat; and the poor little robins, and blue-birds, and humming-birds, he had only killed for the pleasure of seeing them flutter down from the boughs where they were singing sweetly—down to the ground, with their broken, bloody wings.

Rodocanachi threw his game aside, and then lay down himself to drink from a pretty stream that ran bubbling and sparkling under the shady trees. He was so thirsty, and had such a monstrous swallow, that, before long, the stream stopped flowing, and, wherever the sun fell into its bed, the pebbles began to grow white and dry. He had drank it almost up, when the giant said to himself, "Bah! what a shallow river, and how the pebbles get into my teeth! I must have a drop of wine to take away the earthy taste."

There, under the shady trees, Rodocanachi drank and smoked, till his head grew hotter than ever, and so confused, that he stretched himself upon the grass; and, while trying to collect his thoughts, fell fast asleep.

Then, how the fairies flew into sight! Down they swung, from all the high oaks and elms, on rope-ladders made of spider-web; and, from under the broad mulleins, up they poured in a swarm; from the other side of the stream they fitted up rafts of pond-lily leaves, and came floating across; for, after the giant turned away, the river had run full again. What had seemed beds of fernleaves came marching down from the hill-side, or out from the deep shade,—they were fairy armies, with banners all astir; and such a rustling as they made, and such a patter of little feet, and flutter of tiny wings, and singing and shouting of soft, glad voices, you never heard!

Last came the car of the fairy queen, a pearly pond-lily, lined and fringed inside with gold, with a golden seat, and drawn by six bright-blue dragon-flies, that sprinkled a light from their transparent wings, as the car shed fragrance all along its way.

The queen arose and lifted her sceptre; which was tipped with a diamond so bright it shone like a star, and could light a path at midnight through the densest wood. She stretched this wand forth, and the noisy multitude grew so still—so still that you could not hear a sound, except the giant's breathing;—then she spoke:

"The time we have watched and waited for so long, so impatiently, has come; the wicked Rodocanachi is in our power at last. Say, what shall we do with him, my subjects?"

Then swelled forth a breeze of little voices, so confused that you could not tell one from another; and the queen's wand rose again.

"We have not a moment to waste, be still, and hear the advice of my general."

"If I have led your armies bravely, O, great queen—"

"Yes, yes," interrupted the queen, "but what shall I do with Rodocanachi? I'll praise you, and receive your compliments afterwards."

"Suffer me, then, to go alone, and, with my spear, this tough acacia-thorn, put out the giant's eyes."

The fairy shook her head, and turned to a statesman, the greatest in all her kingdom:

"What say you?"

"Cut off his hands and feet, and make mince-meat of them, as he made of my cousin's family!"

Again the queen shook her head, and turned to a grave judge, the wisest man in Fairy-land:

"Let us go together, and, while he sleeps, roll this old sinner off from the mountain-top, that his bones may be well broken when he reaches the valley below!"

At this the little people all shouted for joy, and some ran towards Rodocanachi, impatiently, to begin; but the fairy, with her sparkling sceptre,

3

called them back.

Puzzled and sorrowful, great queen as she was, she wrung her little hands and wept. "I cannot bear to do such cruel deeds," she sighed; "and yet how shall I banish this tyrant, and make my people happy? O, I wish any one, who thinks it a pleasant thing to be a queen, could stand in my place to-day!"

CHAPTER II.

DANDELION.

In the court of the fairy queen was a child, as pretty and gentle as a flower; a little boy, whose work it was to gather dew and honey, and bring it to his mistress in an acorn-cup, or strewn in separate drops over some broad leaf.

Now, this child loved his mistress dearly, and his heart was large and true as if it had beat in a larger bosom; he could not bear to think of torturing even the cruel Rodocanachi,—much less could he bear to see his dear queen grieve.

Little fellow as he was, he tried to make his way toward the fairy's chariot; but the people crowded so, and moved their banners about so restlessly, that more than once he was thrown to the ground, and trodden under their feet.

But Dandelion—that was his name—caught at the tip of one of the fern-leaf banners, which happened to lean toward him; and, when it was lifted into the air, he swung himself, like a spider, from banner to banner, over the heads of the crowd.

Then he climbed up among the pearly, perfumed lily-leaves of the fairy's car, and, all powdered over himself with gold-dust from its splendid lining, knelt at his mistress' feet.

The queen smiled through her tears,—for she was fond of Dandelion,—and asked why he had come at such a time; then said: "Perhaps my pretty one can give me some advice." And all the fairy-people laughed at the thought of a poor little boy being wiser than statesmen and generals.

Dandelion did not care how small they thought him, if he could but help his queen; so he said, bravely:

DANDELION TICKLES THE GIANT'S NOSE.

"O, my great mistress, I was shaking dew out of the cups of white violets that grow by the stream, when this giant lay down near me and fell asleep. Then all the people hurried, and I with them, to your court. I heard you ask what should be done with the wicked Rodocanachi; and, when no one had an answer to give, and my mistress sorrowed, I crept back all alone to the hill-top, where the giant lay, and climbed on his shoulder—"

"My brave little Dandelion!" said the queen.

"I had picked up a feather, that a wood-dove had just let fall on the grass; and with this I tickled Rodocanachi's nose—"

"Fine work!" growled the general. "Suppose you had wakened him, and we were all slaves again!"

But the queen, waving the general back to his seat with her sceptre, said, "Let the boy go on: I am curious to hear the rest."

"The giant stirred; his head was on uneven ground, and the great brass helmet tipped, tipped, tipped, and at last it rolled away, and left his forehead bare."

"O, Dandelion, you have saved my kingdom!" said the queen; and the people all shouted "Bravo!" and "Hurrah for Dandelion!" as, without waiting longer for leave, they rushed to the hill-top where Rodocanachi lay.

Then came a clanging sound, as if all the mountains were great brass drums, and twenty giants were beating them—it echoed so far and wide.

"Ah, it's the giant's helmet! and now we fairies are safe!" exclaimed the queen. She clapped her hands, and the six blue dragon-flies flew to the hill-top with their chariot in time for Dandelion to see the helmet, still jarring where it had been thrown by the fairy-people, far down among the rocks.

"Now, fly, fly quickly," said the queen, "and tear up sods and bushes, and gather leaves, till you've hidden the helmet so safely that Rodocanachi can never find it again."

Fairies, though little people, are not slow; and when at last the giant, with a snore that sounded like thunder, awoke from his sleep, the helmet, for which he began to look at once, was nowhere to be seen.

And the giant's strength was gone. He could not break the stem of a wild-flower, much less lift the game he had killed that very day. He could hardly totter home; and, when there, could not open his own door.

So Rodocanachi began a search for his helmet: all in vain, in vain. He stepped his great feet into it, and never guessed it was hid underneath the grass, and bushes, and flowers, that looked as if they had always grown where they were.

For a year he wandered up and down the earth, growing thinner and sadder every day. He had nothing to satisfy his monstrous appetite except berries and mushrooms. Sometimes the fairies, in pity of his wretched state, would crack a handful of nuts, or kill a frog or two, for his breakfast; but Rodocanachi fairly starved and worried himself to death.

And the queen was so grateful to dear little Dandelion, that she made him always dress in cloth-of-gold, and gave him a beautiful golden shield.

But this was only to remind the people how he looked when the boy crept up into her chariot that day, all dusted over with gold. When Dandelion died, a plant sprang out of his grave,—and every one said the fairy put it there,—that had blossoms exactly like his golden shield; and, when these withered, there came globes of seed, with starry wings, that could fly about in the air, and swing on the wind, from leaf to leaf, as Dandelion swung on the fern-leaf banners once. We call the flowers Dandelions, to this day.

When, in summer-time, you see these golden shields sprinkled over the meadows, and along the roadsides, you must think of the brave little fairy, who did great things because so willing to do the best that he could.

———————————

CHAPTER III.

MINNIE'S HOME.

We have found, from the history of Dandelion, that no one is too small to be of use. We have found that kind hearts may succeed where wise heads and strong arms fail; but perhaps you will wonder what Rodocanachi has to do with my story.

I'll tell you. Have you forgotten that I began to describe a beautiful little town, with roads that wound about like rivers, and houses set in the midst of garden-beds?

Great hills rose on every side, folding against each other as if they meant to shut out the rest of the world, with its noise, and trouble, and weariness. So the valley looked, from a distance, like a bird's nest lined with moss, and leaves, and long fine grass; and the houses and churches seemed like white eggs scattered among the greenery.

Or, if you stood in the centre, the slopes of the hills were so smooth and round, that the valley was like the inside of a painted bowl:—here were woods and waterfalls like pictures; here meadows of grass and grain; white patches of buckwheat, and the tender green of oat-fields, were striped along with brown potato-beds, and patches of dark-green tasselled maize.

In this gay-painted bowl, in this soft grassy nest, lived a little girl, whose name was Minnie, and whose history I mean to tell.

But what has it all to do with Rodocanachi?

Why, this: people say that the beautiful valley between the hills was nothing less than the inside of the giant's great brass helmet! Rivers had found their way through it now, and forests had rooted themselves on the sods that were spread by fairy hands; yet, deep down underneath, the helmet still was wedged among the rocks. Think what a giant Rodocanachi must have been, when you could thus put a whole town into his hat!

Whether the wonderful place in which she lived had anything to do with Minnie's strange history, I cannot tell. See what you think about it.

The house of Minnie's father was near the centre of the town, and in a street where there were many other houses. These were not joined together in a block, like city dwellings, but each had a garden and summer-house, and a patch of grass in front for the children's play-ground.

Around Minnie's house was a curious fence, made of thin strips of iron, bound at the top with a square board, painted white.

In the next house lived a boy named Frank. He was a bright, good-natured little fellow, just of Minnie's age, with rosy cheeks and curly hair, and as full of fun as he could be.

Minnie herself was very fond of play. Perhaps she played too hard, for she did not look hearty and rosy like Frank, but was slight and quick as a humming-bird, and fluttered about so from one thing to another, that it was more than her mother could do to keep her always in sight.

One minute she'd be seated quietly on the door-step, looking at the pictures in a book; the next she was away, and you only caught sight of her curls going round the corner of the house.

Or, perhaps, after you had looked for Minnie in the garden, she would start up with her laughing eyes from behind your very chair, and the next instant she was fluttering along the top of the fence, standing on one foot, and, with her bright pink dress, looking more like a flower than a little girl.

The iron strips of the fence were so far apart that Minnie could easily peep through, and could even crowd her little hand between the squares, to stroke Franky's curls, or pat his rosy cheeks.

As soon as breakfast was over, every morning, both Minnie and Frank would run to the fence, and talk and play there for hours.

But Minnie was not satisfied with this; she wanted to swing on the boughs of her father's young fruit-trees, and, as I told you, would climb the fence, and skip along the rail upon one foot.

Again and again her mother warned her that she might fall and kill herself, or at least soil and tear her dress, and that it was rude for little girls to be climbing trees and fences.

It was of no use. Even while she was talking, Minnie would clamber into some place so dangerous that her mother would have to run and take her down.

CHAPTER IV.

MINNIE AND THE SQUIRREL.

One day, when Minnie's mother had been telling her how wicked it was to be so disobedient, and how much trouble she gave every one that loved her, the little girl thought she never would climb another fence, but would begin now, and be good.

So she seated herself on the door-step, and was quiet as many as two minutes.

Then a little brown sparrow came hopping, hopping along the top of the fence, and stopped a short way off, and chirped, as if he were saying, "You can't catch me!"

"Can't I?" said Minnie, and another minute she was dancing along the rail.

The sparrow flew away, and then Minnie, remembering the promise which she had made to her mother, went back to her seat.

She was quiet longer this time, for she began to think how hard it was to be good. Then she remembered how the sparrow had flown away—away off alone up into the bright blue air, and could sing as loud as he chose, and tilt on the highest boughs of the trees, and nobody call him rude.

And the sparrow didn't have to be washed and dressed in the morning, and to eat his breakfast at just such a time, and be careful to take his fork in his right hand, and not to spill his milk.

O, how much better breakfasts the sparrow had! First, a drink of dew from the leaves about his nest; then, a sweet-brier blossom to give him an appetite; and then, wild raspberries and strawberries, as many as he wanted; and, afterwards, wild honey to sweeten his tongue, or smooth gum from the cherry-tree to clear his throat before the morning song!

Then for a merry chase through the woods, instead of going to school. "O, dear! O, dear!" said Minnie, "why wasn't I made a sparrow?"

Just then she heard a chattering in the pine-tree over her head, and a squirrel tripped in sight. Minnie happened to have some nuts in her pocket, so she quietly rolled one along the top of the fence, and squirrel came down for it.

I think wild creatures know which children are their friends, and which their enemies. At all events, this squirrel did not feel afraid of Minnie, but sat there nibbling at the nut she gave him, until he had eaten out all the meat.

Just then her mother came to the door with some ladies, who had been making her a call, and off darted squirrel, quicker than you can think.

"Now, where has he gone?" thought Minnie; "down under the cool grass, I suppose, or far off into the pleasant woods, where he can have all the nuts he wants, and play hide-and-go-seek among the boughs. O, dear! I wish I had been a squirrel! I wonder if I couldn't run along the fence as quickly as he did just now!"

Her mother was talking so busily with her friends that she forgot to watch Minnie, and off the little girl flew, along the rail, skipping and dancing, and twirling upon one foot.

And now comes the wonderful part of my story. Minnie thought she heard somebody scream, and then she looked round, and her mother was gone, and she was seated on the door-step all alone again, and squirrel, on the fence beside her, was eating his nut.

"Come, give us another!" he said, at last, throwing away the shell, and speaking with the queerest little squeaky, grumbling voice.

"Why, who taught you how to talk?" asked Minnie, in surprise.

"O, nobody. Squirrels don't go to school. They couldn't keep us quiet on the benches, you see. It makes us ache to sit still!" and he ran round and round the rail of the fence, to rest himself.

"Pray, don't go away yet," called Minnie; "I want to know if all squirrels talk, or what you did to learn."

Down the squirrel jumped into the grass, pulled the blades apart with his paws, and smelt of this weed and that, till at last he found what seemed to satisfy him, for he broke off a sprig, and went back to his seat on the fence.

"Minnie, how should you like to live with us?" he said. "We have good times, I tell you, out in the woods. We do nothing but chatter, and eat, and fly about, all day long. We haven't any master, and the whole world's our play-ground; the deep earth is our cellar; the sun is our lamp and stove."

"But I should frighten the squirrels, I'm so large!" and Minnie stood on tip-toe, to let him see what a great girl—as indeed she was, beside a squirrel!

"The same weed that made me talk like a little girl, will make you grow small as a squirrel. Do you dare to taste it?" and he tossed the green sprig into Minnie's lap.

"Dare? yes, indeed! who's afraid?" She ate the leaves at a mouthful.

CHAPTER V.

A SQUIRREL-BACK RIDE.

Minnie had only half believed what the squirrel said, and was surprised and almost frightened when she felt herself growing smaller in every limb. Did you ever drop a kid glove into boiling water? It will keep its former shape, but shrink together so as to be hardly large enough for a doll. Thus Minnie's whole form shrank, until she was no taller than squirrel himself, and not half so stout, and her hands were as tiny as his paws.

"Now we'll have plenty of fun," said squirrel; and they started together for the woods.

But Minnie walked so slowly, with her little feet, that her guide soon lost his patience. He would dart on out of sight, and come back for her, again and again; he would wait to eat nuts, and dig holes in the ground to bury some against winter-time; and still Minnie, for all her hurrying, lagged behind.

At last squirrel said, "This will never do; seat yourself on my back, and I'll carry you faster than any steam-car that ever you saw. Here we go!"

It was a pretty sight—the little rider and her frisky steed, bounding so gracefully over the road. They had not gone far, however, when Minnie called,

"O, squirrel, pray, pray stop!"

"What's the trouble now?"

"You go so fast it takes away my breath, and the underbrush all but scratches my eyes out; and the grass is full of bugs and ugly caterpillars, that stretch their cold claws to catch at me as I go past."

"Is that all?" He darted by a post, along the fence-rails, and up the trunk of a tree, and into the leafy boughs. But now it was the squirrel's turn to complain.

"Don't pull at my ears so hard! Why, my eyes are half out of my head! It is bad enough to carry such a load!"

"But, dear squirrel, I shall tumble off! Here we are, away up in the air, higher than any house, and you skip and leap, and scramble so, it frightens me out of my wits."

"Jump off a minute, then; I know a better way to carry you."

No sooner had Minnie obeyed, than he was out of sight. With one spring, he had leaped to the bough of a taller tree;—and now would he ever come back?

It made her dizzy to look down. It seemed further than ever to the ground, now, she had grown so small. And the insects that crept and flew around her looked so large! A great mosquito came buzzing about with his poisoned bill, and then a hard-backed beetle trolled past, and two or three fat ants. And a bird alighted on the bough, and began to sing.

Minnie drew down a broad leaf to hide her face, for she felt afraid that the bird would think her some kind of bug, and eat her up. Perhaps he meant to do so, for he kept hopping nearer and nearer as he sang.

"O, how I wish I were at home!" thought Minnie. "Perhaps my mother is looking for me now; and Franky has been standing ever so long at the fence, with the half of his cake that he promised to save for me. How could that old squirrel be so wicked as to leave me here alone?"

Still the bird hopped nearer, and eyed her as he sang, and looked as if his mouth were watering for a taste.

"I shall be killed and eaten up by ants and worms if I fall to the ground," thought Minnie; "or, even if I reached it alive, I could never, never find the way home, with these small, slow feet. Let the robin eat me, then."

But now came a rustling amongst the leaves, and a chirping, chattering sound, and, lo! her friend the squirrel frisked into sight. He seemed to be quarrelling with the bird, for she half spread her wings, and stretched her beak as if she could bite him; and squirrel chattered and chuckled at her, and his bright brown eyes flashed with anger, till the robin flew away.

"A moment later, Minnie, and you would have been changed into a song. That saucy fellow meant to eat you for his luncheon," said squirrel. "Now, don't complain that I went away; if you do, I shall go again. We never allow any grumbling out here in the woods."

"Yet they allow quarrelling, and murder, and mischief of many kinds, I see," thought Minnie; "but as I've come so far, I will not go home without learning how birds and squirrels live."

CHAPTER VI.

LIVING IN A TREE.

The squirrel now tucked his little friend under his chin, as if she were a nut, and off they went together, fast as any bird could fly.

Minnie soon found there was no use in urging squirrel to go in a straight line, and pick out the smoothest paths: it was not his way. He made her dizzy, often, by running along the under side of the boughs, or twirling round them in his frisky way; and, in passing from tree to tree, whichever branches were farthest apart, they were the ones he chose for a leap.

If he heard with his quick ears any sound that frightened him, down squirrel darted into some hollow trunk, that was full of ants and rotten wood, and wiry snails; but Minnie found he was growing very tired, and was all in a perspiration with carrying such a burden; so she did not complain.

Yet, when, in passing, her curly hair caught on the rough bark, and had many a pull, and her cheeks became bruised with brushing against the leaves, and she shook black ants and beetles out of her dress, Minnie more than once wished herself home again.

At last, with a chuckle of delight, squirrel darted up the trunk of a beautiful elm, and seated Minnie where the great boughs parted into something like an arm-chair; while he went to find his mate.

This, then, was her new home! Tired and hungry as she was, the little girl looked about her with pleasure—it was such a lovely place. On one side were sunny fields; on the other, stretched the silent, shady wood, with its beds of moss, and curtains of vine, and clumps of wild-flowers.

Closer about her, fanning her warm cheeks, were the green leaves of the elm —more thousands of them than she could think of counting, and all so fresh, and creased, and pointed so prettily. "Many a game of hide-and-seek I'll have here!" she thought.

But now squirrel returned with his wife, who shook hands with her little guest very politely, and begged her to feel quite at home. Madam Squirrel was not so handsome as her husband, but was such a kind, motherly person, that you would not notice her looks.

She had brought some dry moss from her nest, and with this made a soft bed for Minnie to rest upon while she prepared dinner. The good soul even wove the twigs together into a leafy bower above her head, and called one of her young ones to stand near and keep the flies away, so that Minnie might have a nap.

The young squirrel, however, was less thoughtful than his mamma. He had so many questions to ask, and so much news to tell, that sleep was out of the question. And Minnie found that the wonderful herb had not only made her grow small as squirrels, but at the same time had taught her to understand their language.

And not this alone; by listening carefully, at first, she could soon make out what all the creatures around her were saying—the bees, and birds; and grasshoppers, and wasps, and mice.

Even the leaves she saw talked to each other all day long; the wind had only to come, and make them a call, and start a subject or two—then there was whispering enough! And the grass underneath whispered back, and perfumed wild-flowers talked with the grass, and the river talked to the flowers, or, when they would not listen, talked to its own still pebbles.

The sun, if he did not speak, smiled such a broad, warm smile, that any one could guess it meant, "I know you, and love you, friends!" And at night the silent moonshine stole into the wood, and kissed the leaves till they smiled with happiness, and kissed the flowers till the air was full of perfumes they breathed back to her, and kissed the brook till all its little wavelets sparkled and laughed together for joy.

Meantime the stars were winking at each other, to think they had caught the cold moon making love!

CHAPTER VII.

MASTER SQUIRREL.

No sooner had young Master Squirrel taken up his stand by Minnie's couch, than he began to tell how fortunate she was in having such friends.

"Yes," Minnie replied, "I was thinking of them this very minute, and wishing I could send word to my dear mother that I was safe. Poor Franky must be tired of waiting for me by this time; there's no one else to play with him. And then, if you could only see our baby; she's so sweet and cunning!"

"Nonsense!" said Master Squirrel; "she is not half so cunning as you are, now. I was speaking of your new friends, my father and mother."

"Well, what about them?"

"O, we belong to such a fine family, and are so much respected here in the woods, and my father is so rich!"

Minnie laughed. "Who ever heard of a rich squirrel? Where do you keep your money? Are there any banks in the woods?"

"Banks enough, but they bear nothing except grass and violets. We are not so foolish as to put our wealth into pieces of white and yellow stone. My father may not have gold, but he has more nuts and acorns hidden away than any other squirrel in creation. As for the silly birds, they never save anything, and the worms and beetles live from hand to mouth."

"What happens to the frogs and flies?"

"O, they creep into a hole, when winter comes, and freeze, like stupid flowers, till the spring sun is ready to thaw them out again. You see, we squirrels are the only wise and prudent creatures. And to think that, among all squirrels, you should have become acquainted with the richest one—you are very lucky!"

"If all your father's nuts were brought together and measured," said Minnie, "how many bushels would there be?"

"What do I know about bushels? He has at least as many as would make a wagon-load!"

Master Squirrel said this with a great air, but Minnie only laughed. "My father does not pretend to be rich, but he gives away more than a wagon-load of nuts every year; besides keeping all we want for ourselves."

Dear children, as Minnie looked upon the squirrel's nuts, that made him feel so important, just so God's angels look upon *our* treasures. Money, fine horses and carriages, are to them no reason for being proud. They smile at our gains and savings, which seem foolish toys to them. The angels have better wealth.

The squirrel was silent, and so ashamed that Minnie said, to comfort him:

"I should not mind never seeing a nut, if I were as bright and spry as your father; and, whether she were rich or poor, I know any one as kind and generous as your mother would always be respected."

"Poh! it is easy enough to be kind. I've seen one ant help another home with his dinner; I've seen a ground-sparrow, when her neighbor was shot, feed the hungry young ones left in the nest; but that's nothing—that doesn't give one a place in the best society!"

"I don't believe the little orphan-birds waited to ask if their friend belonged to the aristocracy. But, Master Squirrel, what do you call society?"

"I will show you, to-morrow. I heard my mother say that she should give a grand party in honor of your coming. Though it will be like my parents (who are very condescending) to ask some of the common people, you may expect to see along with them all the aristocracy of the woods."

Now the mother-squirrel came with Minnie's dinner; and, sending her talkative son away to give invitations for the party, busied herself with spreading out the tempting meal.

Of course there were nut-meats in plenty; walnuts on one leaf, chestnuts on another, and ground-nuts and grains of wheat on a third. Then there was a bit of honey-comb, and a ripe red strawberry that squirrel had run a mile to pick on the mountain-top; and there were some slices of what Minnie thought must be squirrels' tongues, they were so small and tender; she ate them with a great relish.

Then squirrel brought, in a nut-shell, a drink of fresh water from the brook; and, filling her shell again, dropping in a sweet-brier leaf or two to perfume it, she bathed Minnie's forehead till the tired little traveller went fast asleep.

CHAPTER VIII.

NIGHT.

Upon awaking, Minnie was surprised to find all dark about her. The good old squirrel had tucked the moss of her couch together so nicely that she was warm and comfortable; but, on reaching out a hand, she felt the leaves wet with dew.

Then a wind stirred the branches, and far up in the sky she saw the twinkling stars, and knew that it was night.

Night, and the little girl was alone there out of doors! No mother in the next room listening to see if her children breathed sweetly, and all was well; no sister Allie to nestle close beside her, now; but the great lonely sky above her, and the creaking elm-bough for her cradle.

And how high this cradle lifted her into the air! She hardly knew which was farthest off, the ground or the sky. It was all so strange that Minnie thought she must be dreaming. She stretched her hands out in the starlight; they were small as squirrels' paws,—ten times smaller than even baby Allie's dimpled hands,—small as those of her smallest doll. Who ever heard of such hands for a little girl?

Yes, she felt sure it was a dream; but, turning to sleep, she was aroused by a loud snoring. Could a man be hidden up here among the boughs? And suppose he should catch her alive, and shut her up in a cage, to be advertised, and talked about, and pointed at with canes and parasols in Barnum's museum?

But now the snores seemed changing to sounds more like the purring of a cat. Were not tigers a kind of cat? Suppose this were a tiger, ready to spring down and seize her in his great paws, as a cat might seize a mouse!

No; there came next a loud, rough laugh, startling to hear in the silence; and then a great flutter, and a scratching sound, and something alighted on the bough above her—something heavy, for the bough bent till its leaves were crushed upon her face.

As soon as Minnie could push the leaves apart she looked up, and saw to her dismay two great round eyes staring full at her! She covered her own eyes, and in her terror would have fallen from the tree, had not her dress been caught among the leaves.

"What's that? What's that?" a gruff voice called.

19

Then Minnie remembered what she had heard her mother, and even the little squirrels, say, that it is foolish to fear anything; so, as loudly as she could with her trembling voice, the little woman shouted:

"How do you do, sir? It's a fine evening, all but the cold!"

And, venturing to look once more, she saw what a curious animal she had addressed; with the eyes of a man, he had the face of a cat, and the bill and body of a bird.

"Who's here? who are you?" was his only answer.

"I am a traveller, sir. I have come from my home in the village, to make my friends, the squirrels, a visit; perhaps I shall have the pleasure of meeting you at their house."

"Not so fast! I'm an owl, I'd have you know, and do not keep company with chattering squirrels. If you wish to see me you must come to my own home."

"And where is that?"

"In the hollow around on the other side of the elm. We owls are satisfied to sit thinking over our wisdom, and do not go scrambling about like squirrels, and other simple creatures."

"How did you happen out to-night?"

"O, every evening I come up on this branch to take the air, and study astronomy."

"Astronomy?—what's that?"

"It is counting the stars, and telling how they move, and watching when they fall. I expect to catch one, some day."

"What shall you do then?"

"Hide it in my nest, to be sure, until I can plant the seeds, and raise another crop."

"Hide a star in an owl's nest! Why, the stars are worlds," laughed Minnie.

"O, that is what ignorant people say. This, that you see above your head, is a huge tree with dark leaves, and hung all over with golden oranges. When the stars seem to move, it is only the boughs that are waving; when the stars seem to fall, it is ripe fruit that drops to the earth. Let me catch one, and you'll see what a fine orange-bush I'll grow from the seed!"

"I'd sooner fly out, in the pleasant morning sunshine, and pick up strawberries, blueberries, checkerberries, all the nice things that grow in the wood," said Minnie; "but, if you can't be happy without the stars,—"

20

"I never can!" exclaimed the owl.

"Then I would fly up where they grow, and pick them myself from the boughs;—not sit in a dark hole, and wait for them to fall."

But the owl—who thought no one's opinion worth much, except his own—could not agree with her, and flew away.

Then Minnie, tired of talking so long, fell asleep once more, hoping, with all her heart, that she should awake in her little room at home, with Allie's rosy cheek pressed close to hers, and her mother stooping to give them both her morning kiss.

CHAPTER IX.

THE NEW HOME.

Cool air and pleasant music were about her, when Minnie awoke the next day, but no home. She was wrapped in a bundle of moss, on the elm-bough, still.

The bright morning sunshine lay over the leaves, fragrant odors came stealing out from the wood, and wreaths of beautiful white mist floated above the brook, and, slowly rising, reached, at last, and melted in with those other white clouds far up in the sky. Yet the lower end of the mist-wreath rested still upon the brook, so that it seemed like a long pearly pathway, joining the earth and heaven.

Many birds had their nests in the elm, and they were feeding and singing to their young; or, floating up in the sky, still kept a close watch over their little homes among the leaves.

Minnie found she had plenty of neighbors. The tree was like a town, filled with people of all colors, and sizes, and occupations. Of course, these were only birds or insects; but Minnie had grown so small that they looked monstrous to her. The birds were as large as herself, you remember. Little lady-bugs seemed as big as a rabbit does to us, and fire-flies were great street-lanterns; butterflies' wings were like window-curtains; bees were like robins; and squirrels, as large as Newfoundland dogs!

As her friends did not come to bid her good-morning, the little girl thought she would go in search of them. She felt afraid to move, at first, but found soon that the bough was as wide for her small feet as a good road would be for larger ones; so, steadying herself now and then by help of a twig or leaf, she wandered on.

Sliding carefully down the slope of a bough, she found herself, at length, close by the entrance of the squirrel nest. Her friend, the young squirrel, was just sweeping the door-way with his bushy tail; but, when he took Minnie in to see his brothers and sisters, she did not find their home a very orderly place.

She could not step without treading on empty nut-shells, bits of moss, or broken sticks; then the place was dark, and did not have a clean, sweet smell, like her mother's parlor. In one corner lay a heap of young squirrels, some so small you could put them into a nut-shell—others larger, and larger still. The nest was so cold and damp that the poor little things had crept together to keep warm.

22

Master Squirrel said, by way of excuse, that his mother was so busy, preparing for the party, she had not been able to set her house in order this morning; but Minnie never afterwards happened to go there when it was in better order than now.

"Where is your mother?" she asked.

"In the woods, at some of our other houses; for we squirrels don't live always in one place. She is gathering nuts and all kinds of goodies for our supper, and will scold me well if I have not the table set when she comes home."

"O, let me help you!"

Squirrel was glad to accept her offer, and they went to work in earnest. First, Minnie insisted upon bringing all the young ones out into the sun, when they stretched out their little heads and paws to receive the pleasant warmth, while Minnie returned to see if anything could be done with their disorderly home.

She sent squirrel into the woods for some pine leaves, and of these made a broom as large as she could handle. Then she swept, and dusted, and brushed black cobwebs down, and wiped the mouldy walls, and put fresh leaves in place of the musty moss on which the children had laid.

By this time the old squirrel had come back from the woods again; and told what a beautiful place his wife had found for their feast, and how glad she would be of Minnie's help. He limped a little, and said his back ached still from carrying such a load the day before; but, as there was no other way for the little woman to reach the ground, she might go with him, only be sure not to pull his ears!

No sooner said than done. Down the trunk of the tall tree they went with a leap or two, and along the stone walls, over bushes, through hollows, further and further into the wood, till they came to a lovely spot.

CHAPTER X.

IN THE WOODS.

A number of trees stood so closely together that they seemed like a solid wood; but, when the squirrel had made a way for Minnie to pass under the heavy boughs, she found inside a circle, covered only with fine soft grass and moss, a few wild flowers nodding across it, and the leaves, with their low, pleasant rustle, closing around it like a wall.

"Now," said the old squirrels, who were too wise to be proud and boastful like their son, "now, Minnie, you know better than we what is proper, and you must tell us how everything shall be arranged."

Nothing could please Miss Minnie better than this. Her mother had not even allowed her to go into the supper-room before company came; and here she was to order all things, and be herself the little mistress of the feast!

They decided to have their party in the afternoon, because at that time the sunshine always slanted so pleasantly through the wood. If they waited till evening, the dew would begin to rise, and there was no depending on the moon for light; and their children, besides, would be needing them at home.

First, Minnie said, they must have a more convenient entrance to the supper-room. On one side stood a large azalea, or wild honeysuckle, in full flower, and near it a sweet-brier; between these were some whortleberry bushes, around the roots of which last Minnie made the squirrels burrow till she could drag them away.

Then, smoothing the broken earth, she covered it with sods of fresh moss, while overhead the sweet-brier and azalia met in a beautiful archway of fragrant leaves and flowers.

And it was so much prettier to have flowers growing in the ground than if they had been cut and brought from some green-house! Both Minnie and the squirrels were delighted with their dining-hall.

Next they spread shining oak-leaves for a table-cloth, which was better so than if it had all been in one piece, because now, wherever a tuft of violets grew, or any of the slight starry flowers that dotted over the grass, they could remain there, and save the trouble of arranging vases.

Then came a great variety of food,—nuts, honey, grain and berries, apple and quince seeds, bits of gum, and strips of fragrant bark. Minnie was shocked when she saw among the game a dish of dead ants, and one of frogs' feet, and another of red spiders; but the squirrel said she must have something to suit all tastes, and the birds would be disappointed if they had not animal food.

Then she begged Minnie to slice some cold meat for her, and brought a big black beetle to be shaved up like dried beef, and an angle-worm to be cut in slices for tongue.

"O, dear!" exclaimed Minnie, as the little round slices of this last fell into the plate, "can this be what I mistook for tongue, and relished so heartily last night?"

"Very likely," squirrel answered; "it is one of the tenderest meats we have."

Minnie resolved to eat no more dainties in the wood, until she had first found out their names; but she had not time to grieve much over her mistake, for the father-squirrel came to tell that he had promised his oldest children a race in the woods, and invited her to make one of the party.

She was glad to take lessons in running of such a quick little body as he; and, while his young ones frisked and bounded, and chased each other, he was very patient in teaching her all his arts. Before many such lessons, Minnie could balance herself on the most uneven and unsteady place; could climb slippery boughs, skip without stopping over the crookedest places, and even leap from branch to branch, so nimbly that squirrel was proud of his pupil.

He would not let her go very far that day, because she must be fresh for the afternoon, when his guests would come.

CHAPTER XI.

THE SQUIRREL'S PARTY.

In due time the company arrived, and all were in such good spirits, and so polite, that Minnie thought she had never known a more charming party.

On each side of herself sat the birds; a blue-bird and yellow-bird first, then a thrush and an oriole, then—cunning little creatures!—a wren and an indigo-bird. The robins and bobolinks were not invited, because they were such gluttons. The crows could not come, because they were so quarrelsome, and the cherry-birds were too great thieves.

Then came a whole row of squirrels, that sat with their bushy tails up in the air, and paws folded quietly, notwithstanding the nuts before them, while they made themselves agreeable to the meek mice and moles, that were all a-tremble, not often finding themselves in such grand company.

One large gray squirrel came in his rough hunting-coat; but he talked so loud and boastfully, and seemed to look down upon all the others with such contempt, they were not sorry when he said, at last, that he had promised to take a walk with his distinguished friend the rabbit, and must therefore go home.

Several toads were invited, and Minnie had even taken pains to roll some round stones into the room for their seats. They came, and were chatting gayly, when their eyes, that wandered over the delicious feast, fell upon the dish of frogs' feet, and home they hopped at once, offended. It was a great mistake, on the squirrel's part, to bring such guests and such a dish together; for who could be expected to relish seeing his cousin chopped up into souse?

The butterflies came, but declined taking seats at the table, as they never ate anything. They fluttered above, with their beautiful velvet wings, and clung to the flowers, bending them down with their weight; and, when Minnie observed how wistfully the birds were eying them, she thought perhaps the butterflies had a better reason than they gave for keeping at a distance.

After eating all they wanted, squirrel proposed that his guests should go to the brook for a drink. It was not far, and Minnie had swept the path nicely with her broom, and spread new moss wherever the ground was bare; so they seemed to be walking on a strip of green velvet carpeting, as, two by two, they started for the water-side.

Some little green, graceful snakes followed on from curiosity, while over the heads of the party fluttered all the butterflies; and a rabbit, chancing to see them, very politely asked squirrel if he might join the guests.

Meantime the toads, that had crept into a corner to mutter about their insult, hopped back to the table, and, along with a swarm of flies and ants, and greedy robins, crows, and bobolinks, soon finished all that the company had left.

CHAPTER XII.

BY THE RIVER.

A yellow-bird was the companion of Minnie's walk, and a pleasant little man he was, with his gayly-spotted wings, his graceful manners, and musical voice.

The oriole was handsomer, and had a sweeter song; but he was proud, and spoke in a sharp, short way, that was not agreeable. Minnie said to herself, "I can listen to oriole while he sings at the top of the tall elm; but for my friend I will choose some one with gentler behavior, if he hasn't so loud a song." Do you think Minnie was wise?

Yellow-bird was equally pleased with his companion, and very ready to converse. He told her that he had often wished to become acquainted with some of his neighbors in the village, but dare not trust them.

"Why?" Minnie asked.

"O, one of my brothers, after eating the plant that makes us wise, heard a little girl·begging him to come and live with her. She promised a beautiful cage in the summer-house, and plants to eat and drink."

"And he went?"

"Yes; he was so unwise. Before the end of a week the little girl had forgotten to feed him, and he lay dead in the bottom of his cage."

"Yet that was an accident; the little girl was sorry, I am sure."

"Her sorrow did not bring him to life again; and I could tell sadder stories— O, too sad stories for to-day!" Here yellow-bird stopped talking, and breathed forth a low, mournful song.

The squirrel, hearing him, turned quickly: "This will never do! Why, friend, we're going to a feast, and not a funeral; pray give us some gladder music."

"Excuse me, I never can sing so soon after eating," said yellow-bird, who was not willing to leave his new friend.

As for Minnie, she had never stood so near a bird before in her life; and could not be satisfied with looking into yellow-bird's round eyes, and stroking the soft feathers on his neck. She had a hundred questions to ask; and he answered so graciously that she began to think she would rather live with those gentle creatures, the birds, than with her kind, but wild and frisky friends, the squirrels.

You may remember it was Minnie's wish at first to live like a bird, on that morning—how long ago it seemed to her now!—when she had sat on her father's door-step, and watched a sparrow soar into the sky, and sing.

They had not time for many words before reaching the water, which in one place spread to a little pond beneath the trees, and reflected the leafy branches on every side, and the sky, with its pearl-white clouds, and the sunshine that lay across it like a path of gold.

An aged birch-tree, uprooted by the wind, had fallen into this pond. Its large and handsome boughs were still alive; and here flew oriole at once, singing as he alighted, and swung on the tip of a branch. The other birds followed through the air, except Minnie's friend, who walked quietly on with her. The squirrels bounded in a trice across the broad, white trunk of the tree. The mice and the moles followed them, and the rabbit was not far behind. The butterflies chose to hover above the sunny water in a flock.

Then squirrel made a speech, thanking his guests for the honor they had done him in spending so much time at his poor feast. He was glad it had been in his power to make some return, by presenting to them so distinguished a guest.

The rabbit took this compliment to himself; so he replied by assuring squirrel that the obligation was all on the part of his guests. In ending, he regretted that he had not chanced to meet earlier with such pleasant companions; the truth was, he had only an hour ago been able to rid himself of a gray squirrel, a rough, unmannerly fellow from the backwoods, whom he would have been ashamed to bring into such polite society.

"Ha!" said squirrel, forgetting his dignity as host, "the very chap that honored us with his presence a little while, and boasted about his mighty friend, the rabbit."

Rabbit folded his ears together very wisely at this, and replied: "A person who feels it necessary to boast of his friends, is never much in himself. Now, *I* always feel that I'm as good as any of my acquaintance."

"I wonder which is worse vanity," thought Minnie, "to boast of one's friends or one's self!"

But here yellow-bird hopped upon a spray, and sang a delightful little song in honor of their fair guest, whom he compared to a flower, a little cloud, a soft willow-bud of the spring-time, a white strawberry, and many other things in which birds delight.

The company were so pleased that they begged to hear the song again,—all except rabbit, who, finding his mistake at last, hopped further in among the leaves, and hid himself, feeling very much ashamed.

Then yellow-bird, instead of repeating his first song, sang another, which was sweeter still. It told how full the world might be of love and happiness, how many such good times as this all creatures might have, if they would but be gentle and kind, willing to please, and ready to forgive.

As the last note died away, oriole, impatient to show his skill, remarked that yellow-bird's song was too much like a sermon; and, without waiting for invitation, he then gave what seemed to him a better one.

And it was enchanting music. O, so clear, and wild, and joyous, that it made the other birds lift their wings, and long to fly!

Hearing a plunge in the water near, and a sigh of pleasure, Minnie looked down between the branches, and saw a handsome green frog, that had come to listen to the music; and swarms of little fish, with rainbow-colors on their silver scales, all listening too.

So the afternoon passed in speeches and music. The squirrels, who could not sing, told stories that made the company laugh right heartily. Even Minnie took her part in the entertainment, by relating how people in the village lived, how they ate, and drank, and slept, and why they did many things which had puzzled the birds and squirrels amazingly.

All this was as interesting to her listeners as it would be for us to read Robinson Crusoe, or Dr. Kane's travels among the icebergs and Esquimaux.

Repeating their thanks to squirrel, and each one politely urging Minnie to visit him, the company now went home.

Yellow-bird insisted upon taking Minnie on his wings, but soon found the little woman so heavy that he was satisfied to let her dance along by squirrel's side, and flew off to find his young. He had, too, a world to tell his mate about the merry feast, and the queer little lady in whose honor it was given.

I am afraid all the birds and squirrels that were at the party kept their mates or their brothers and sisters awake that night, relating what they had seen and heard. Even the mice talked about it in their cellars under ground; and oriole did not sleep a wink, he worked so hard composing a song to Minnie's eyelashes.

CHAPTER XIII.

THE YELLOW-BIRD.

At daybreak the next morning yellow-bird came with the indigo-bird and thrush, and awakened Minnie with their charming songs. Sunrise, you know, is the time birds always choose for serenades; and I am not sure they are wrong—everything is so fresh, and still, and dewy, then.

She could hardly wait till the music was over before shaking away the moss in which she had slept, and going to bid her friends good-morning. Skipping fearlessly along the boughs,—for she had not forgotten squirrel's lessons,—just as the birds were preparing to fly away, Minnie surprised them with a sight of her merry face.

They did not chat long, for Minnie could see that her friends were impatient for their morning sail up in the fresh blue air. So she begged them to fly away, while she would go to the squirrel-nest and find if breakfast was ready.

She met squirrel, who, though much fatigued, and sometimes obliged to put his tail before his mouth in order to hide his gapes, was as civil as ever, and bade her a pleasant good-morning.

His wife did not happen to be in so amiable a mood. Not only was she tired from all the work and anxiety of the day before, but Minnie's sweeping and dusting, she said, had put everything out of order in her nest. Besides this, the children had taken cold from staying out of doors so long, and the light of the sun had given them weak eyes.

Minnie was troubled, and offered her help in making things go right again.

"No," Mrs. Squirrel replied, "I have had enough of such help, and now you can best assist me by keeping out of the way."

This was very rude, and brought tears into Minnie's eyes. It was bad enough, she thought, to be so far from home, but to be treated unkindly, and after she had worked so hard in hopes to please the squirrel, this was more than she could bear.

Running so far from the nest that she could not hear the angry voice within, Minnie seated herself on the bough, and, all alone there, thought of her pleasant home, and the mother who was so ready to praise her when she did right, and just as ready to forgive her when she did wrong. She seemed to see Franky looking through the fence, waiting, and wondering if she would never come. Then she saw Allie open her large eyes, and, peeping between the bars of her crib, look all about the room, and stretch her little hands forth for Minnie, and no Minnie there!

Even if she went back now, would they know her, shrunk as she was to a mere doll? Before she could reach her father's door, wouldn't the boys in the street pick up such a curious little being, and put her in a cage, or sell her, perhaps, to be killed and stuffed for some museum?

"O, I haven't any home, or friends in all the world!" she said, and, covering her face with her little hands, Minnie sobbed as if her heart would break.

"Hallo, there! what's the matter?" shouted young Master Squirrel from the bough above. "It can't be you're crying because the old woman is cross? Why, she'll be good as chestnuts by the time you see her again. Here, catch these nuts! she made me crack them for your breakfast."

Minnie thanked the squirrel, but she could not eat. Her heart was too heavy. She hoped that, when the birds came back, they would not find her, for she was too much grieved to talk, or even listen to music.

She had hardly drawn the leaves about her, when she saw the indigo-bird, and then the thrush, making their way towards the elm. Minnie held her breath, while they alighted and hopped from bough to bough, and turned their heads on one side to peer between the leaves, and sang little snatches of song, that she might hear and answer them. At last they flew away, and when oriole came, he had no better success.

Then came yellow-bird, with a fresh ripe strawberry in his mouth. He also looked in vain, until, just as he was lifting his wings to go, his quick ear caught a sigh, so low that only loving ears would have heard it, and he flew at once to Minnie's feet.

She still held the leaves fast, and yellow-bird was obliged to tear them with his beak before he could be certain that she was within.

"Poor little soul! what is the matter?" he said, when he saw her sad face, wet with tears.

Then Minnie put her arms around yellow-bird's neck, and told all her troubles. He did not speak a word until she had finished, when he exclaimed, "You shall not live with the squirrels any longer. Come to my own warm little nest on the other side of the elm. My mate will be glad to see you, and you shall have sunshine and music all day long. Tell me, Minnie, will you come?" He ended with a little strain of song, so sweet and pleading that Minnie could have kissed him for it, only, you know, a bird's mouth is rather sharp to kiss. She pleased him better by promising to go that very hour to his nest.

CHAPTER XIV.

IN A BIRD'S NEST.

Yellow-bird's nest was all that he had promised. It was built on one of the outer boughs of the elm, deep enough among the leaves to be shady at noon, yet not so deep but in the cool of morning the sunshine could rest upon it.

Then the view was much finer than that from squirrel's side of the tree. Minnie looked down upon fields of wild flowers all wet with dew, across at hills that rose grandly against the sky; and, better still, between the trees she caught a glimpse of the town, with its white spires and cottages.

It was an important day with yellow-bird, for a whole brood of young ones were leaving his nest for the last time. He had taught them to sing and fly, had shown them where to find food, and given so much good advice, that now he did not feel afraid to trust them by themselves.

He brought his children to see Minnie before they left, made them sing a little song of welcome and farewell, and then watched with pleasure as they flew into the wood, and soon were lost amid its shady boughs.

Minnie asked if it did not make him sad to lose his treasures all at once.

"O, no," he said; "if one of my chicks had been blind, or had grown up with a broken wing, and could not leave the nest, I well might grieve. Now that all has gone well, I'm only too glad to see them fly away."

"But suppose that, when out of your sight, they fall into trouble or mischief?"

"They are never out of God's sight. Cannot he take better care of them than a little bird like me? Ah, Minnie, it isn't best to fret! The smaller and weaker we are, the more care our heavenly Father takes of us."

Yellow-bird's mate came now to see what her husband could be talking about, and invited Minnie to take a nearer look at her nest, which she had been industriously cleaning and mending since her children went.

It was a smooth, cool bed of horse-hair and moss, set prettily amidst the thick green leaves. Slender roots and threads were woven across the outside, and what was Minnie's delight to find among them a scrap of one of her mother's dresses, which yellow-bird said he had picked up beneath a window in the village, for it was so soft, and covered with such bright flowers, he knew it must please his mate!

Minnie felt that the nest would be dearer to her, and more like home than ever now. Yet she knew it was not civil to leave her good friends, the squirrels, without a word of good-by; so, lighter-hearted than when she left it, she skipped back to their den on the other side of the tree.

She found the old lady's temper very much improved, perhaps because she had her nest in what she called order again. Minnie tumbled over nut-shells, tore her dress against thorny sticks, and, when she stretched her hand toward the wall, trying to rise, she felt cold mushrooms growing out of the crumbling wood.

It was dark, too,—no prospect there,—and there was the old musty odor, which she remembered so well, instead of the sweet air and fresh green leaves above yellow-bird's nest; and there was the heap of sleepy young squirrels squeaking in a corner.

"O, dear!" thought Minnie, "how could I ever have wished to live in a place like this?"

Mrs. Squirrel was polite once more, and kindly offered her some luncheon, but did not ask her to stay. And, though surprised, she did not seem grieved when the little lady told her that she had come to say farewell.

Not so squirrel himself, who was proud of Minnie, and fond of her, and felt so badly at parting, that his lips trembled too much to bid her good-by, and he ran off into a hole in the ground to hide his tears.

"Dear squirrel! he has done the best he could for me," she thought; "and now, because he doesn't happen to have a pleasant home, I am about to leave him! I have a great mind to go back!"

Just then a nut-shell dropped on her head, and, looking up, she saw Master Squirrel, who laughed at her surprise. Leaping a little nearer, he began:

"So you've returned, Miss Runaway! My mother said it would be too good luck to lose you in a hurry. She was sure we should see you before the sun went down."

"Then your mother doesn't like me?"

"O, yes! she says you're a cunning little body, and mean no harm; but, like all company, you make a great deal of trouble, and do no one any good, that she can see."

"What does your father say to that?"

"He takes your part; tells her he's ashamed that she is not more hospitable; and then they quarrel well, I tell you!"

"There shall be no more trouble on my account," said Minnie, with dignity. "I am going to live with my friends, the yellow-birds. I have bidden your father and mother good-by, and now good-by, squirrel; you have all been very kind to me."

"No we haven't, Minnie; and I have been rudest of all; and you, so good, to be satisfied with our poor home!"

"Dinner-time! plenty of checkerberry buds and juicy berries in the wood!" sang yellow-bird on a bough above. "Come, Minnie, come!"

"Good-by, squirrel! Yellow-bird, here I am."

"O, Minnie!" was all the answer squirrel could make. She left him wiping his eyes on his hairy paws—left him, and skipped away with her new friend.

CHAPTER XV.

MINNIE AND THE BIRDS.

For a little while Minnie was very happy with the yellow-birds; they were gentle and loving as the days were long, and only disputed to know which should have the pleasure of doing most for their company.

At home it was all sunshine and music, exactly as they had promised; and, when there was too much sun, they flew to the wood, where hundreds of other birds met also, and merrily passed the long, bright afternoons.

It was like a party every day. Instead of needing to set a table each time, there was the whole wood, with its flowers, berries, gums, and spicy buds, spread out for them to take their choice. The wine bubbled up freshly from their cellar, and spread into bright wells wreathed with flowers. No need of corkscrews and coolers; yet, the best wine in the world never tasted so good, nor left such clear heads, and such merry, thankful hearts, as this simple water —the only drink the birds asked at this woodland feast.

Minnie made friends among great and small, she was so sprightly, and ready to please, and so willing to be pleased herself. This last is a great secret in winning friends. If people find it hard to amuse us, they very soon grow tired of trying, and leave us to entertain ourselves.

But Minnie had a pleasant word and a merry answer for every one. She did not laugh at the oriole for his foolish pride, nor at the ant for her stinginess and silence, nor at the bee for making such a bustle, nor at the indigo-bird for her diffidence. She knew it was their way, and only took care not to imitate their faults herself.

Meantime she never was tired of admiring their better traits of character. Let the oriole be proud as he would; she knew that hardly any one else could sing such lovely songs as he was always twittering. Let the ant be ever so mean and dumb; who else had such an orderly house, and such a store of food? Let the bee buzz; couldn't he turn the poorest weeds into delicious honey, and set it in waxen jars of his own making, yet so neat, and delicate, and well contrived, that any man or woman might be proud of them? Let the indigo-bird be shy; once hidden among the leaves, wasn't she willing enough to trill forth the clearest, loudest, sweetest little songs?

Ah! in this great wide world there is no creature but has some precious gift for us, if we can only find it. The little bird is weak, but his voice can fill the whole sky with music. You may know some rough boy who seems wicked;

but be sure there's a good spot in his heart, and, by treating him kindly, we may make that good spot larger. Isn't it worth while to try?

Though yellow-bird, after giving many lessons, found he could not teach Minnie to fly, he taught her so much that, by resting one hand on his neck, she could easily glide along with him through the air.

In this way they fluttered from bough to bough in the wood, then took longer flights through sunny meadows, and at last ventured up among the clouds, where Minnie had longed to go.

Up, up, they soared,—yellow-bird singing for joy,—till there was nothing around them except the bright blue air, and, close over their heads, rose the pearly morning clouds.

Many a time had the little girl sat on her father's door-step, and longed to be where she now found herself. Many a summer morning she had watched these same clouds gather and wrap themselves together, till they looked like splendid palaces of pearl—pearly domes and spires dazzlingly bright in the sunshine, and porticos with pillars of twisted pearl; and, at little openings, she could look through vast halls, all paved with pearl, and curtained with silvery hangings.

At sunset the roof of her beautiful palace had changed from pearl to silver, and all its spires were gilded; the silvery hangings changed to rose-color; the floor, instead of pearl, was paved with solid gold, and the pillars were made of shining amethyst.

"O," Minnie had thought, "if, instead of this little house, with its dull, iron fence, I could live in such a noble home as that, how proud and happy I should be!"

Then, as a man passed, with his ladder, to light the street-lamps, she wondered if hundreds of ladders tied together couldn't reach as far as the clouds.

"How I would skip up the rounds," she thought, "and, when I had reached the highest, send my ladder tumbling back to earth! The ladder would break, so no one could follow me; and all day long I'd fly from hall to hall, or, through great winding staircases, find my way to the golden cupolas, where I could look down into the poor old dusty earth I had left."

And now, without tying a hundred ladders together, here she was among the clouds. Alas! the pearly halls, that from below had looked so beautiful, were damp and dismal vapors. It was chilly and lonesome up there, while, wonderful to tell! the earth seemed a warmer, sunnier, more cheerful place than she had ever known it. There was the pretty town, with its surrounding hills and woods, with its winding rivers, and green fields, and tranquil lakes. In all the sky there was nothing half so beautiful!

CHAPTER XVI.

THE SQUIRREL'S TEAM.

After the long sky-journey, Minnie was glad to reach her home in the elm once more. She was weary, wet, cold, and disappointed. She longed for the blazing fire in her mother's room, and the warm, pleasant drink her mother could mix for her. She longed to hear Frank's merry voice, and to see baby Allie with her golden curls.

There was no use in longing. Even if yellow-bird should fly with her to the very window, they wouldn't know her. They would only laugh at the curious little creature she had grown, and hang her up in the cage with their canary-birds. So she would make the best of her home that was left, and not distress her kind friends by wearing a gloomy face.

She was trying to smile, when a pleasant chirp told her that the yellow-bird's mate was near. She soon hopped into sight, and, welcoming Minnie in her kind way, told that she had an invitation from no less a person than his majesty, the owl.

The party was made especially for Minnie; so she could not refuse, although it was to be held at midnight. Yellow-bird would go with her.

"And you, too?" Minnie asked.

"Excuse me, dear, this time. I feel obliged to stay at home."

"So do I, then."

"Ah, I will tell you a secret. I have in my nest some of the prettiest little eggs you ever saw. If I should leave them they might be chilled with the night-air; so never mind me, Minnie, but go and have the pleasantest time you can."

"To tell another secret, then," Minnie answered, "my dress is not only worn to rags, but so soiled that I am ashamed of it, and cannot think of going into company. See what a plight!" And she held up the skirt that was torn into strips like ribbon.

"Is that all? I watched to-day while a cruel boy was shooting in the wood. He fired at a poor little humming-bird, and broke its wing. It fluttered down among the bushes, and lies there now, I suppose, for I took care to call the boy away."

"How?"

"O, we understand. I cried out as if he had also wounded me; and, when he

39

began to search, went slyly round into another place, and cried again. So I led the boy on, till I felt pretty sure he could not find his game if he went back."

"But why did you take so much pains?"

"Partly so that he should not carry the pretty little creature home, and send half the boys in town out here, next day, hunting humming-birds, and partly because I thought the feathers would make you such a warm, handsome cloak. Fly with me, now, and we'll find it; for here comes my mate, to take his turn in staying with the nest."

They quickly reached the bush, under which humming-bird lay dead; but how heavy he was! It was as much as ever Minnie could do to lift him from the ground.

While they stood over him, wondering what was next to be done, Master Squirrel frisked in sight, rolling before him a large, round turtle-shell.

"Stand out of the way!" he shouted. But Minnie stood across his path, and, for fear of throwing her down, he stopped; and, leaning on his shell, not very good-naturedly asked what she wanted.

"O, squirrel, do leave your play a little while, and help us!" she said. "We have this heavy bird to carry home, and skin, and make the skin into a cloak, while the daylight lasts; do be kind, now, and help us!"

"It isn't my way to be kind; but I'll make a bargain with you."

"Well."

"Yellow-bird shall fix a harness out of straw, fasten you into my shell for a horse, and I will drive home with your load."

"That's a good plan," said Minnie, not waiting to think how squirrel had kept the best of the bargain for his own share. "What say you, yellow-bird?"

"Poor little woman! after such a long journey you are too tired to drag this great fellow home. I will do it myself."

"Then I will help you twist the ropes."

To work they went, and soon had the harness finished. Squirrel, meantime, selected a good long twig for a whip, laid the humming-bird across the shell, and leaped into his place.

He could hardly wait for the harnessing to be ended; but Minnie made him stay until he had promised only to snap his whip in the air, not use it on yellow-bird, and they darted on.

CHAPTER XVII.

THE MOONLIGHT DANCE.

Minnie tripped behind, watching the little team. She had grown so nimble that she could keep nearer than squirrel thought.

When he supposed he was out of sight from her, he lifted his whip, and gave yellow-bird a smart stroke across his shoulders.

But she knew how to punish him;—spreading her wings at once, she rose into the air, and made the deceitful squirrel roll out of his chariot.

He was ashamed to see Minnie after this, so limped away, whining that he had broken his paw, and would tell his mother.

Then yellow-bird sung one of her droll little songs, that were like twenty laughs shaken together, and, when Minnie came, begged her to take the squirrel's place, and drive home.

The little woman was too thoughtful of her kind friend for that. She went behind and pushed, while yellow-bird dragged the shell, and they soon had it safe beneath the elm.

Then they slipped off the humming-bird's skin in a trice, hung it a while on the sunny side of the elm to dry, and Minnie's good friend pulled out from among the twigs of the nest that dear piece of her mother's dress, and gave it to her for a lining.

You never saw a prettier and more fairy-like little garment than this when it was finished; the tiny feathers all lay together so evenly, and whenever the wearer moved they took such brilliant hues! Now the cloak was red, now brown, now green and gold, and again it glittered with all these colors at once.

Minnie had always seemed like a bird, with her quick, light, flying ways, and more than ever she seemed one now, with her gay feather cloak, and the fluttering, sailing motions she had caught from yellow-bird.

Mrs. Yellow-bird, having put the last stitch in Minnie's cloak, fastened it about her neck, and looked at her guest with great satisfaction. Then, at a chirp, her mate came, and readily consented to be Minnie's escort; so away they flew together.

The evening was mild, and clear moonlight filled the wood. Owl had chosen a lovely green dell in which to meet his friends, and had fitted it up with taste, and no little pains. All among the bushes and lower boughs of the trees he had tied live fire-flies and bright green beetles. He had built for the dance a tent of bark, and had sanded the floor with a curious dust that is found in the wood countries, and is like pale coals of fire.

The birds dared not step on this fiery carpet at first, for fear of singeing their feet; but owl assured them that it had no warmth. As for the fire-fly lanterns, it must be confessed that the birds' mouths watered in passing them, but they were too civil to eat up their host's decorations.

There was an orchestra of crickets, and they played such merry tunes that the guests all danced and waltzed till they were tired, and then it was supper-time.

Alas! owl had not been so thoughtful as the squirrels, and had only furnished such food as he liked himself. You may judge the surprise and disgust of the company, when, to the music of the band, they were marched in front of a heap of dead mice!

The owl began to eat at once, and begged his guests not to be diffident. Not one of them tasted a morsel, however. Some politely refused, some went home angry, and a few had the courage to own that they were not fond of mouse-flesh.

Thus owl's party ended, and, indeed, all his parties, for, the next time he sent out invitations, every bird in the wood respectfully declined.

If we think of no one but ourselves, we shall soon be left to ourselves.

CHAPTER XVIII.

THE LITTLE NURSES.

Minnie almost fell asleep on her way back to the elm, and found it hard to keep up with yellow-bird, who flew on briskly as ever.

Her long morning journey, the labor and hurry of making her cloak, as well as the effort to bring the humming-bird home, and the party afterwards, the dancing and late hours, tired her so much—so much that she feared all the rest in the world would not make her strong again.

And when the tree was reached, Minnie's friends did not, as usual, offer her their nest. They must keep it now for the eggs. Cold and weary as she was, the little girl must lie down among damp leaves, with no other bed than a mossy place which she found on the rough bark of the elm.

In the morning she still felt tired, lame, and stiff, yet her spirits came back with the sunshine, and when she told yellow-bird she had not strength enough to fly away with him, he stayed and sung to her a while, and afterwards brought her delicious berries from the wood, all sweet and ripe, and cool with dew.

With such an attentive friend to supply her wants, it was not very hard to sit quietly upon her couch of moss, so green and velvety, with sunshine all about her on the leaves, and the pleasant prospect below.

You will remember that the tree was full of inhabitants, and our Minnie had made friends with almost all of them. When well and active, she had never passed them without a pleasant word, or at least a nod of welcome; and, now that she was sick, they were most happy to sit and talk with her, or offer their assistance.

They brought her presents, each in his kind. The bee came up from among the clover-blossoms, to place clear drops of honey on the leaf beside his little friend. The silent ant stopped a moment to tell the news, and presented a morsel of sugar which she had hoarded in her nest till it was brown with age. Indigo-bird brought a berry, blue as his wings. Some of the birds brought good fat angle-worms or snails, which would be dainty morsels to them. These Minnie laid aside for her friend Mr. Yellow-bird, although she thanked the givers politely, as if what they brought were her own favorite food.

This was not deceitful, because what Minnie enjoyed was the thoughtful kindness of her friends, and not their gifts. The berries were sweet, to be sure, but their friendship was sweeter.

Master Squirrel came among the rest. He and a spider of his acquaintance had made Minnie a beautiful parasol, with the humming-bird's bill for a handle, and a wild rose for the top.

The pink cup of this flower, turned downward as it was, cast such a glow upon Minnie's pale face, that Master Squirrel thought he had never before seen her look so handsome.

Soon, tired of listening to his coarse compliments, the little girl asked what else it was that he kept so nicely covered in his hands.

"O, that's my mother's offering!" he replied. "How the old woman would have scolded if I had forgotten to give it to you!"

"Pray, let me have it. How kind your mother always is!"

"Except when her nest is too clean, eh? Well, she saw me working over the humming-bird's carcass, and thought, as the meat was fresh, perhaps you'd like a scrap cooked for your dinner."

"Cooked meat! O, I haven't tasted a morsel since I left my father's house!" said Minnie, in delight. "Where could your mother have found the fire, though?"

"Not far off the woods are burning,—took fire in the dry season, as they often do,—and there were plenty of coals; so madam cut off the humming-bird's wing, and broiled it—O, my!—till it smells so nice that it made my mouth water to bring it to you!"

He lifted the cover, and there, on a green leaf, lay the dainty wing, all crisp and smoking now. Minnie relished her dinner more than words can tell.

CHAPTER XIX.

MOUSE.

Before Minnie was strong again, yellow-bird's eggs hatched, and both he and his mate were busy and anxious, all the time, with taking care of their nest full of little ones. She did not see her friends so often as formerly, and, when they came, their visits were hurried and short.

And, one by one, her other acquaintances grew forgetful, for birds and insects don't have such good memories as we, you know. Each was occupied with his own cares and amusements. Perhaps the truth was that they had grown tired of Minnie, as you grow tired, in time, of your prettiest playthings.

She felt all these changes. She remembered sadly what Master Squirrel had said, that his mother thought company a great deal of trouble, and herself, though a cunning body, of no use to any one.

What if yellow-bird and his mate should begin to feel the same? She determined not to stay and trouble them any longer, after they both had been so kind; but where in the great world could she go for a home? Who would feed, and comfort, and love her? Ah! how sadly she remembered the dear mother who had made it all her care to watch over and supply her children's wants!

Every creature in the wood had a home and friends, except herself! And yet none of these homes were so pleasant, none of these friends so sweet and loving, as the ones she had foolishly thrown away.

"Ah!" thought Minnie, as in the dusky twilight she lay swinging on a lonely bough of the elm, "Ah! if I could whisper loud enough for every little boy and girl on earth to hear, I'd say, 'Be happy in your own home, with your own friends; for there are no others like them—none, none, none!'"

Though these sad feelings were weighing on the heart, the rocking of the bough and sighing of the evening wind among the leaves lulled Minnie soon asleep.

She awoke in a terrible storm. She was drenched with rain, which pelted like pebbles, in sharp, quick drops, beating the leaves, while the wind dashed the boughs together, and made Minnie fear that, though clinging with all her strength to the branch, she must fall.

And she did fall into the wet grass far below, and was stunned, perhaps, for she did not awake until morning.

45

Then the sun shone brightly once more, the elm above her glittered with sparkling drops, and the first sound which Minnie heard was yellow-bird's song of joy that his little ones were safe after all the wind and rain.

"He has forgotten me, or he would not be so glad!" she whispered to herself. Then came the thought, "Perhaps he is happier because I am swept away out of his sight!" and with this she began to cry.

"What's the matter?" asked a little mouse, that was running about in the grass, picking up worms and flies which had perished in the rain. "What's the matter? Have my proud cousins, the squirrels, been treating you badly again?"

"No, they all do more for me than I can do for them; but, dear little mouse, I've stayed in the woods too long. Every one is tired of me. Couldn't you show me the way back to my mother's house?"

"Why, Minnie, *I* am not tired of you. Pray, don't go home yet. Come and make me a visit in my snug little hole, so quiet underground. No storms reach there. I shall not whisk you about as squirrel has done; nor take you long, weary journeys through the air, like yellow-bird. I'll bring you cheese, and meal, and melon-seeds, till you grow rosy as your little sister Alice."

"My sister! What can you know about her, pray?"

"Wasn't I at your house this morning? I have, not far from this very wood, a passage-way underground that leads into your mother's pantry. Come to my nest, and you'll hear news from home."

CHAPTER XX.

HOUSEKEEPING.

Minnie gladly followed the mouse into his hole. To see some one who had been in her dear lost home, was almost as good as to feel her mother's gentle hand laid on her head once more.

In the promised news she was disappointed! Alas! the mouse disappointed her in many things. Minnie had not lived with him long before she found that she had fallen into bad company.

He was good-natured and hospitable in his way, but a sad thief, and his word could never be depended upon. The little girl even felt afraid of her own safety, when she saw what pleasure mouse took in betraying all who trusted in him.

The first time she fell asleep, the mischievous fellow nibbled off what rags were left of her gown, to make a bed for his young. Minnie feared that next he might pick out her eyes for their luncheon, and determined to leave him before it should be too late.

But it seemed as if the sly mouse saw into her mind, for, as she was composing her farewell speech, he came running out in the grass where she had seated herself, and said, in his squeaking voice, "Minnie, will you do me a great favor?"

"I shall be glad to do anything in my power," was the reply.

"Well, you didn't seem satisfied with the news I brought from home, and so I have resolved to go and try if I cannot pick up some more."

"I suppose you won't pick up any of my mother's cheese and pie-crust?" said Minnie, laughing.

"Of course not; at least, not more than enough to pay for my trouble in going. And now, Minnie dear, I want you to take care of my little ones while I'm gone,—to feed them, and see that they don't roll out of their nest."

"That I will do very willingly."

Mouse scampered away, and Minnie little thought how long it would be before she should see him again.

The nest was narrower, deeper, and darker, than squirrel's, and quite as close and disorderly. It was hard for Minnie to crowd herself through the entrance; but, once within, she found paths winding in every direction, some of them

47

ending in little chambers. Part of these rooms were store-houses of grain, cheese, and all manner of rubbish, which mouse must have stolen for the pleasure of stealing, Minnie thought, it was so wholly useless. The other rooms had each its brood of little mice, of all sizes and ages, some almost as large as the mother, some not much larger than a fly.

It took the whole afternoon to wander from one room to another, explaining where the mother had gone, comforting those that began to fret, feeding the hungry, quieting the quarrelsome. Glad enough was Minnie when she had tucked up the last brood in their bed of wool, and could creep out into the grass for a breath of air and a look at the pleasant sky.

Shaking the earth from her cloak of humming-bird feathers, and picking a handful of checkerberries, Minnie looked about for a stone to sit upon while she ate her supper.

She soon found one, smooth as any pebble in the brook. Here she could eat at her leisure, while a band of crickets and katydids played to her, and all the beautiful stars twinkled over her head, and all the grass about her was strung with glistening drops of dew.

"After all," she thought, "this is more to my taste than being shut up in my curtained bed at home. What's the use in stars and dew, if we never look at them? What use is there in the evening breeze, if we shut it out with our windows? It's a good thing to have our own way, and I may yet be glad that I left my father's house."

CHAPTER XXI.

TROUBLE FOR MINNIE.

As Minnie sat meditating, suddenly the grass about her seemed to move. The long blades bent this way and that, and shook their dew-drops over her.

What could this mean? Had the grass feet? Could it draw its roots up out of the ground and walk?

Why, *she* was moving! The grass behind lay bowed together in her pathway, and here she was, seated close under an evening primrose, which opened its yellow blossoms so far from the mouse-nest that she had only felt their fragrance when the wind blew.

Presently something like the head of a great snake was stretched out from under her seat. Minnie sprang up at once, and, climbing into the primrose branches, wondered if she were awake or asleep, that such strange things should happen.

Then the snake's head disappeared, and a low voice spoke from under the stone, "Why do you leave me? I live in a pleasanter place than the mouse, and am myself more honest and agreeable. Will not the little woman make me a visit?"

"Why, what's your name, and where did you come from? and are you a stone, or something alive? and is that snake's head a part of you?" said Minnie, half frightened, and half amused.

"What you are so polite as to call a snake's head is my own, and what you call a stone is my shell, and I am a turtle, Miss Minnie," the voice answered, with dignity.

"Pray, don't be angry with me, turtle; I meant no harm. Now the moonlight has come, I can see the beautiful golden stars on your back; and, now my fright is over, I remember what a pleasant ride you took me through the grass."

"You shall have as many such rides as you want, if only you'll come and stay with me by the side of the brook."

Here was the very opportunity Minnie had wished, to find a safer home; but she could not forget her promise to the mouse, and leave the little ones to suffer.

When she told turtle this, he said that she was perfectly right, and, creeping back with his load to the entrance of the nest, and finding the mouse was still away, he left Minnie, promising that by sunrise in the morning he would return for her.

Accustomed as she had long been to the shelter of the elm-leaves, the dampness rising from the ground made Minnie sneeze so violently that the crickets stopped playing to listen. She was glad to go, at last, inside of the nest, and sleep in one of the close little rubbish-rooms.

At daylight she was awakened by a small brown beetle running up and down her arm. Rubbing her eyes, she asked, rather sharply, why he could not let her sleep in peace.

"The turtle wants to know why you don't keep your promises. He has been waiting this half hour, and sends word that it is a shame for you to sleep away the beautiful morning hours."

Minnie sprang to her feet at once, and was following the beetle, when squeak, squeak! ho, hallo! wait a minute, Minnie! came from every room she attempted to pass.

She found that mouse had not kept her promise of coming home, and, sending a message to the turtle, she was obliged to wait and hear a hundred questions and complaints, and settle a hundred disputes between the quarrelsome young ones.

One had pushed the other out of bed; one had trodden on the other's tail; one tickled the other so that he could not sleep; one snored so loud it made another nervous; one had eaten up the other's grain.

As Minnie crept about in this dark, disagreeable place, so full of angry voices, she remembered that lost home of hers, where all was peace and love. She remembered dear Franky, with his rosy cheeks and curly hair,—the good, generous little fellow that he was; and baby Alice, with her large brown eyes; and the kind parents who never went away and forgot *their* little ones.

Then she rummaged the store-rooms for food; and, not finding enough to satisfy the greedy mice, crept out into the air to see if she could not pick up something for their breakfast.

She saw no turtle. The grass was bent still with his foot-tracks, but he was gone. So Minnie went busily to work picking off seeds and berries, and the honeyed end of clover-blossoms, till she had such a heap that it seemed to her she could never carry it all into the nest.

Then thinking, "Perhaps, if I set the mice at work, it will stop their quarrelling," she called out several of the elder broods.

CHAPTER XXII.

TROUBLE STILL.

The young mice seemed obedient to Minnie until they had reached the entrance of the nest; but, at the first taste of fresh air, they began to frisk about, and do whatever they chose.

First they attacked her heap of food, and ate all the choicest bits which she had saved for the little ones. Then off they ran, this, that, and every way, Minnie calling after them in vain.

She went in search of the runaways, but they hid safely under the leaves and grass, or burrowed into the ground. Tired and discouraged, the poor girl turned back to collect what food was left, and give it to the little ones.

And still the old mouse did not come home. Minnie wondered if she had gone on purpose to be rid of her family, and if she must herself have the care of bringing up this great brood of noisy, troublesome mice.

Why not let them starve? If they grew up, it would only be to cheat and steal, like their mother, and run away with people's meal and cheese.

Ah! but Minnie had promised. And, besides, the old mouse had been kind in her way, and had offered Minnie a home when other friends forsook her. No, she would not desert the little ones.

All at once she remembered a trap that used to stand in her mother's pantry; suppose the mouse was caught in it! She would go this instant, and see.

Now the underground pathway was very, very narrow, and so close and warm that three times Minnie gave up her attempt, and as many times went back; for, when she thought that the friend who had fed her might be starving, it was enough to drive away all other thoughts.

Still, not being a mouse, she could not breathe in that close cellar-way. Her strength all left her. The little heart, that had beat so fast when she thought of going home, home, only fluttered faintly now. She began to feel that she could not even creep back to the mouse-nest; that this dark passage was to be her grave.

But one step forward brought Minnie into a good-sized room, and what was her surprise to find this the nest of the father-mouse!

He didn't like the noise and trouble of children, he said, and so kept away from the sound of their voices. He hoped his mate was well, and was just on the point of going to see what had become of her.

When Minnie told her fears, he uttered a frightened squeak, and said he was sure she must be right, and that he was a poor, lonesome widower, and should never see his dear, dear wife again.

Minnie cheered him by telling that her mother's trap was not one of the cruel ones with teeth, but only a box with wires, in which his wife might live safely for several days. Then she explained how with his teeth and paws he could open the door and set her free.

Away flew the mouse, first showing his friend a nearer and easier pathway out into the air.

Minnie now began to consider how displeased the mother-mouse would be, on returning, to find her children scattered in all directions. If she could but call them together, and see them safe in the nest once more, bid the old mice good-by, and ride off quietly herself on the turtle's back, how happy she would be!

She climbed the tall evening primrose, and looked on every side, but not a sign of a mouse. She leaped into the grass again, and, with the stick of her parasol, stirred every tuft of clover and bunch of violet or plantain leaves. In vain.

Minnie had made up her mind that they were lost, drowned in the brook, or eaten by some bird of prey, when she caught sight of one, with his bright eyes and sharp little nose peeping up from under a toadstool.

Then she knew that all the rest must be near, and, jumping on top of the toadstool, she said,

"You mischievous fellows, I dare say you are all laughing at me in your hiding-places; but hear this! your mother is dead, perhaps, and as sure as you stay out of your nest at night, some mischief will come to you. I shall waste no more time in this search."

Wasn't it ungrateful in the mice to disobey Minnie, when she had taken so much trouble for their sakes? And yet I have known children whose parents took as much pains for their sake, and who were as thoughtless and disobedient as Minnie's mice.

CHAPTER XXIII.

FREE AT LAST.

When Minnie returned to the nest, whom should she meet but mouse in the midst of her little ones?

The mate was there also. He had come partly to help home his wife,—who had lamed her foot in the trap,—and partly to boast of his wonderful courage and ingenuity in setting her free.

Both were very profuse in their thanks to Minnie; for the young mice had already told of her kindness and care. Minnie interrupted their thanks to ask the news from home.

This, mouse had half forgotten in her flight. She only remembered how, after the trap shut down upon her, the pantry-door had opened, and a lady came in.

"Tell me exactly how she looked," said Minnie.

"She wore a gown of pink muslin, and pink ribbons in her hair."

"O, that was my own mother! How I wish I had been in your place!"

"I wished so too. When she lifted her hand and took down a jar of sweetmeats, that stood close by the trap, I felt sure she'd see me, and have me killed. O, how I trembled! It was as much as ever I could do to keep from squeaking when I thought of my mate, and all the little ones."

"Was my mother alone?"

"No; a little boy came with her, and watched while she took the sweetmeats out into a dish. Before closing the jar, I saw her give him a taste of the delicious pine-apple."

"How did you know it was pine-apple?"

"O, after my mate had set me free, we waited to lap up a few drops that trickled down the side of the jar. We know the taste of good things! Was that boy your brother?"

"No; it was dear Franky, my playfellow, who lives at the other side of the fence. Didn't he say anything?"

"He asked the lady if she supposed Minnie was where she could have nice pine-apple for tea. I couldn't hear the answer, for they both left the pantry then."

"My generous Franky! He always thought more of others than himself."

"Don't cry, dear, and I'll call you my generous Minnie. Think! if you had not been so kind, all our little ones might have starved."

"Yes; and my own wife might have dried up into a skeleton in that dreadful trap!" said the father-mouse. "How glad we are that we have such a kind friend to live with us always!"

Alas, it was hard for Minnie now to tell that she meant to leave their nest! But, hearing the slow steps of turtle brush through the grass above, she thanked the mice for their good-will, and hurried out into the sunshine, to meet her new and faithful friend.

As for the mice, they were so taken by surprise, that at first they could only look after her, without saying a word. But, before she had reached the brook, Minnie heard a squeaking and scrambling underground; and, from a little opening, which she had not seen before, up darted mouse and her mate, trembling with anger, and talking so noisily, both at once, that she could not make out what either said.

Meantime turtle, who had little respect for mice, kept on at his steady, slow pace, through the grass. As Minnie was mounted on his back, the mice were obliged to travel also, in order that she might hear their complaints and reproaches.

For they had forgotten all about gratitude, now, and could only grieve over the missing broods of young.

As soon as Minnie discovered this, she begged turtle to wait a moment, that she might tell her side of the tale; but on he jogged, and, when the mice would not be still, snapped at them so fiercely with his snaky head, that they both scampered home in fright.

They had not grieved for naught. Four of the truants had drowned themselves in attempting to cross the brook; two had been eaten by a crow; and the rest were snapped up at a mouthful, by a spaniel, that happened to run through the field.

CHAPTER XXIV.

TURTLE.

You remember Minnie was a restless little soul; and will not be surprised to learn that she had not lived with the turtle long before his slow ways tired her.

He was stubborn and disobliging, too. If he started for a place, she couldn't make him turn one inch aside; but on, on, on he crept at the same slow pace, —no matter whether Minnie were wet, and half-frozen with rain, or parched with sunshine,—on, on, till he reached his goal.

Still he was always quiet and dignified, had no quarrels with his neighbors, and seemed to treat his little guest as well as he knew how.

It is true he surprised her in disagreeable ways sometimes. If he saw a pool of deep mud by the road-side he would wallow through it, sadly soiling Minnie's fine cloak of humming-bird feathers. She knew he was partial to mud, and would not have blamed him so much had this excursion been all; but, instead of going back to the grass, where she might wipe herself clean, he would mount some slanting log that rose out of the water, and stand there sunning himself for hours.

One day, a gentleman, who was driving past in a chaise, saw Minnie and the turtle perched thus on a log, and stopped to examine the curious object.

Turtle drew his head inside of his shell at once, and left poor Minnie to her fate.

Now it happened that the traveller was a great naturalist, and especially fond of collecting turtles. He had hundreds of them, snapping at each other, and scrambling over each others' backs, in his yard at home.

Still he was always on the watch for a new specimen; and here was a famous one, he thought. Springing from his chaise, the gentleman ran to the other side of the brook, and was walking cautiously toward them, when turtle thought it time to look out for his own safety. So, dropping from the log, he disappeared in the thick, muddy bottom of the brook.

The naturalist went back, disappointed, to his chaise. Minnie, in passing, caught at some iris-leaves, and clung to them. As soon as she could wipe the water from her mouth, she called out, "Allow me to bid you good-by, Mr. Turtle. I think I can take as good care of myself as you've taken of me thus far, and henceforth I will save you the trouble."

"What's that? I'm rather thick of hearing," said turtle, from under the mud.

"Good-by, that's all!" And, by the time he had reached the end of his log once more, Minnie was floating down the brook on a pond-lily leaf, diving every now and then to cleanse herself from the mud which turtle had dragged her through.

"Why shouldn't I live by myself? Where's the use in giving others so much trouble?" she said now. "Why cannot I play with the flowers and butterflies, run races with the ripples, and bright little fishes, in the brook; or sleep on any bank of moss, or in any empty bird's nest that I can find? At least, let me try; and, if I grow hungry or lonesome, there are enough good people to take me in."

CHAPTER XXV.

MINNIE'S WINGS.

Now came the most beautiful and happiest part of Minnie's wandering life. So nimble was she, and ready for sport, and so droll, and withal so gentle and ready to oblige, that she made friends on every side. Wherever she went you'd be sure to find a flock of butterflies, or bees, or birds, about her.

They taught her all the pretty sports which they had practised among themselves; once more she flew across the meadows with the birds, fed on the fresh, clear honey of the bee, and played hide-and-seek with butterflies.

Sometimes the butterflies lifted her far up into the air. How do you suppose they contrived to do it, with their slender wings, which even the wind could break?

Minnie told them that, in her father's house stood a statue, with wings on the wrists and feet. This was Mercury, whom the Greeks in old times worshipped as one of their many gods.

Now, she thought the butterflies might make a little Mercury of her. No sooner had she said as much than a beautiful pair, spreading wings large enough for sails to her lily-leaf boat, floated through the sunshine to settle upon the little woman's shoulders. Then followed smaller ones, with blue, white, and yellow wings; and, fastening themselves to her ankles and wrists, up, up, they all flew together!

But the next day Minnie found her little friends creeping about with their wings sadly sprained. So she would not often let them repeat this experiment.

O, I should have to write a larger book than this to tell you what good times Minnie had with the butterflies; into what pleasant places they were always leading her; how gentle and playful they were, and how their wings were perfumed with the flowers they had lived among.

She loved to have them follow her when she walked, especially that little golden kind you have often seen in the meadows. Some followed, some fluttered on before, as if she were a little queen, and they her body-guard.

There were no angry voices now, no envious neighbors; no Master Squirrel came to repeat disagreeable stories. Instead of that stifled squirrel-hole in the elm, she had the sweet air of heaven about her now. Instead of that crowded yellow-bird's nest, where Minnie had felt in the way, she had now the wide meadow, with room enough in its soft, green lining, for herself and all her friends.

But, alas! Minnie was the one, this time, to cause trouble and discontent. Only to gratify her wilful temper, she did what she would have given half the world to undo afterwards. It was a little thing,—you would hardly call it wicked; and yet it grieved and drove away her gentle friends, and would have cost her own life, but for an accident. These *little things* make half the mischief in the world.

CHAPTER XXVI.

HIDE-AND-SEEK.

One afternoon, tired of playing in the hot sun, Minnie thought she would creep under some shady cluster of leaves, and sleep.

But the butterflies could never have play enough, and the hotter the sunshine, the better for them. So they did not understand that the little girl needed rest, and, thinking her weariness only make-believe, would not give her any peace.

They ran across her hands, they tickled her cheeks with their feathery feelers, they pelted her with buttercups, and at last began to cover her over with leaves of the wild rose. So full of mischief were they, that one could no more sleep, while they were about, than if they'd been so many bees.

At first Minnie tried to be good-natured, and laugh at their pranks; but, warm and tired as she was, you cannot wonder that her patience didn't last.

Some children would have roughly driven the butterflies away—have pelted them with stones, perhaps, and broken their beautiful wings. But Minnie could not forget how kind they had been; and besides, you know, they were not such little things to her as they seem to us; they were almost as large as herself.

She only arose, and, turning her back, would not speak to them, or spoke in such a snappish manner that the butterflies were frightened, and flew away.

Left alone, she espied, near the wood, something that looked like a side-saddle, just large enough for a little body like herself. She sprang to see if there were a tiny horse to fit, and thought how quickly he should gallop off with her, so far that the butterflies could not follow—no, not if they wore their wings off!

But the saddle proved only to be a flower, so much like a wadded leather cushion, that Minnie took her seat upon it, and was swaying back and forth with its tall, stiff stem, when she noticed that it was surrounded by a row of leaves more curious, even, than the flower.

Each leaf was like a little pitcher, with such great ears that Minnie wondered if it were not the very kind she had heard her mother talk about, when she was whispering secrets. There they stood, like the forty jars in which Ali-Baba caught the forty thieves, in the Arabian Nights.

"Here's a place to hide!" She had hardly said it, when the butterflies came in sight, and Minnie slipped into the tallest pitcher, unseen by them, she thought.

But no—they found her; and now was Minnie's time to laugh. Fold their wide wings together, crumple them as they might, not one of the butterflies could crowd himself through the narrow neck of the pitcher. They could only stand and look down wistfully at the roguish face within.

"I'm glad to see you! shake hands!" said Minnie, shaking their slender wrists till they begged her to be still.

"Ah! Minnie, not so rough! Come, now, don't be cross any longer. Come out and play with us!"

"Don't you wish I would? Don't you wish you could catch me?" was all the answer she made.

"But we've found a bee that a bird killed, and we saved the honey-bag for you."

In vain they urged. Minnie was very stubborn. She laughed at the butterflies, and teased them, until they were offended, and, one by one, flew back to the brook.

And, now that she had leisure to look about, the little girl found herself in an uncomfortable place. Not only was the pitcher half full of water, but so narrow that she could hardly move, and lined with stiff hairs, that seemed like thorns to tiny hands like hers. She would not stay here.

But how to escape was the question! She only climbed the sides to slip back again; her arms were scratched till they bled; her garments were heavy with the water in which they drabbled. Night was coming down; she could hear the crickets sing; she caught glimpses of birds flying home to their nests; yet all were so noisy or so busy that they could not hear her voice.

How she wished, now, that her rudeness had not driven the butterflies away! But it was too late for such wishes; they had gone.

CHAPTER XXVII.

MINNIE IN PRISON.

Minnie thought the night would never end. She watched the stars that moved so slowly overhead; she watched the moonlight slant into the wood, and the pale flowers fill with dew. She heard the night wind creep among the leaves; and her old friend the owl, and other wild creatures that hide by day, she heard prowling about in the dark.

Sometimes there would be a quick cry, or a patter of light little feet, or the dull hoot of the owl; and then all was still again, and Minnie gazed once more to see how far the stars had moved. O, it was such a little way, and they had so far to go before the sun would shine again!

At last she fell asleep from very weariness, and awoke to find a faint red light above the eastern hills. It was morning—morning! Another hour would see the sun rise, and bring some friend, perhaps, to help her away from her prison.

When some kind friend awakens you at sunrise on a summer morning, and, feeling drowsy, you long to turn and sleep again, and wish daylight would never come, you must suppose that you were in Minnie's place, and see then if you do not find it easier to spring from your beds. Because the sunshine comes to us so freely, we must not forget how precious and beautiful it is.

Suppose the darkness, instead of lasting for one night, should last whole months, as it does at the far north. What a damp, dismal world it would be! How we should grope from place to place, and, sitting in our houses by the flicker of poor lamps, how we should long for the sunshine—for the beaming, generous light and pleasant warmth that spread now over all the land!

The birds began to rustle among the boughs, or, half asleep still, sing short dreamy songs upon their nests; but Minnie could not make them hear her little voice, and had resolved to call no more, but drown or starve, if she must, when a humming-bird came wheeling and buzzing by.

He was such a noisy fellow himself, that, like the rest, he might have passed on without noticing Minnie's cry, but he paused to drink at the pitcher, where he knew that water was hid; and what was his surprise to find an old acquaintance there!

Minnie was always ready for a joke; so she popped up her head like the little men you have seen shut into boxes, that, when the cover is lifted, start up and frighten you.

She knew very well that if humming-bird flew away at first, his curiosity would lead him back again. She laughed to see how quickly he flitted into the wood, and then how cautiously he came forth, and, from bough to bough and plant to plant, made his way to her side once more.

Then Minnie's face grew serious, as she told her little friend how much she had suffered and feared through the long, long night, and begged that he would help her to escape. He was not half strong enough to lift her, though he tried till his bill ached with dragging at her tangled hair.

And this work, if hard to him, was not, as you may judge, the most agreeable to Minnie. She persuaded the humming-bird to leave her for a while, and see if he could not find help, or, at least, find something for her to eat.

It happened that, in seeking food for Minnie, the bird found something of which he was especially fond himself; so, after eating his fill, he went humming across the meadow, never thinking again of the friend he had promised to help.

Very impatiently the little girl expected him every moment, until an hour had passed, and still she waited, hungry and alone.

Then came a great flapping of wings overhead, and a rustling such as she had once heard when a hawk flew into her father's poultry-yard. He had eaten the white chicken that she called her own, and it was as large as she was now. Suppose he should eat her!

The rush of wings came nearer, and the bird, whatever his name might be, alighted close beside Minnie, who ventured to peep over the edge of her pitcher, and beheld a curious, tall, awkward creature, such as she had never seen before in her life.

She coughed to attract his attention, and he turned toward her a bill as long as her own arm was once, and began to stalk about on legs longer, even, than his bill, and that looked like a pair of stilts.

CHAPTER XXVIII.

NARROW ESCAPES.

"It's a pleasant morning for a walk," Minnie ventured to say.

Her visitor answered with a croak so rough that she couldn't tell whether he agreed with her or not. But, taking a long step, the stork came nearer, and looked directly down into Minnie's prison, and upon the little, tired, mournful, frightened face.

"Pray, don't hurt me! I have lost my way, and fallen into this dreadful place."

"Why do you stay here, if it is not pleasant?"

"O, I cannot climb out, I'm so small; and the sides are so slippery, and all these thorns so rough!"

Then, without waiting to be asked, the stork broke the leaf-stem, and, turning it upside down, shook Minnie out into the grass.

It was so good to stretch herself in the pleasant sunshine, that Minnie folded her hands, and lay there quietly as if she was asleep, or dead.

The stork travelled around her on his stilts, and Minnie heard him say, "In all my flying, I never came across such an odd little creature before; it looks like a woman, yet isn't larger than a bird. Its feathers are like a humming-bird's, and yet they are pretty well worn out. I wonder how it happens!"

With this he began to poke and pull at her cloak; finally, off it came, and stork held it up in the sun for examination. Then he eyed the little silk apron her mother had made, and twitched it by one corner, till Minnie began to think he would eat her piece by piece.

So, the first time he turned his head away, she sprang to her feet, and, without once looking behind, ran, leaped the fences and the fallen boughs, and, reaching her home by the brook-side, hid under the shadow of a stone.

And high above her, she watched the stork beating the air with his heavy wings, and sailing on out of sight.

After eating some savory roots, which the mouse had taught her how to find, and taking a berry or two for dessert, Minnie jumped into the brook, which looked warm and tempting as it rippled through the sunshine.

She could swim as swiftly as any fish, and was so very fond of the sport that she soon forgot her weariness. Laughing and shouting, she started in chase of a swarm of little minnows, whose silvery sides shone like moonbeams when they darted across the brook.

Minnie kept gaining ground, and thought, at last, that she could lay her hand upon the minnows, crowded all together as they swam; but, lo! at the first touch, like so many bubbles of quicksilver, they scattered far and wide. Some shot before her, some dodged behind her back, some hid their silly noses under stones and weeds, thinking, if only their eyes were out of sight, that nobody else could see them.

Of these last, Minnie caught several; but they slipped through her fingers again before she could be certain that she had them there. She might as well have tried to hold one of the ripples of the brook.

Now that the butterflies had forsaken her, Minnie found it lonely in the meadow, and spent most of her time by the stream. When it was low she would trip over the wet, rough stones in its bed so fast that the dragon-flies, with all their wings, could hardly keep pace with her.

And, when the little stream was full to its brim, she would nestle inside of a water-lily, and float for hours, half asleep, watching the sunny ripples pass. In more restless moods, she would climb tall bulrushes, or swing among the long, ribbon-like iris leaves. There was no end to the ways she had of amusing herself.

But one day, when she was swinging, a boy mistook her for a butterfly, and, springing among the iris-leaves, had almost caught her in his hat. Another day, as she was floating in the brook, an angler came, and threw a pretty, gay-winged fly into the water. When Minnie seized this, a sharp hook pierced her hand, and, the next thing she knew, she was lifted high in the air on the fisherman's line! In an instant she freed herself from the hook, and fell back into the water; but it was many days before the wound stopped smarting, and many more before it healed.

Still another time, Minnie found the brook covered with mosquitoes; the fields were parched with the August sun; and the road, where all the birds had gone to chat with the butterflies, was hot and dusty. So the little girl nestled under some cool violet leaves. In the woods violets blossom all the year round, you know, not plentifully as in spring, but here and there you find a cluster in bloom.

Such an one Minnie found, and, when she stretched herself in the grateful shade of its leaves, the sweet flowers looked down at her like the blue eyes of her mother, and the wind, that was whispering through the long, fine grass, seemed her dear lullaby.

But, as she leaned her head on the moss at the violet roots, and thought of home, there came a sudden jar, and the next moment she was rolling in a heap of dusty earth, and vainly striving to free herself, as you have seen ants when their nest was broken open.

A man was digging up the sod of violets to plant on the grave of his little child that was dead. Minnie feared that, if he detected her, he would stick her on a pin, as some new kind of butterfly, for his cabinet. She hardly dared breathe until his work was finished, and the man had gone away.

CHAPTER XXIX.

THE LITTLE SEAMSTRESS.

All dusty and ragged, Minnie stood wondering whither she should turn next, and what would become of her.

No place seemed safe, no friends stood by her long; her garments were torn to fringes, and the hot sun pelted down its rays upon her so that she was faint.

She had barely strength to climb a tall pine-tree near in whose boughs she had often swung, through the long afternoons. But that was in happier days. The sighing of the wind among the branches, which used to be such pleasant music, was so mournful now that it filled Minnie's eyes with tears. It seemed as if a hundred soft, sad voices were calling, just as Minnie's heart called, for her mother to come and fold her in her own dear arms once more, and comfort her, and forgive her, and take her home, never, never to wander or be disobedient again.

"Halloa!" said a voice. "What's the matter this time? Have you lost your fine cloak, or has some one else grown tired of my little woman, and sent her off to starve?"

"Pray, squirrel, don't tease me, now. I'm so homesick, and so poor, and tired, and discouraged, that it seems to me I shall die."

"That's what I said you'd come to, when you left us; but I'm your friend, Minnie, though I am such a rude fellow, and I don't mean you any harm. Good-by!"

Master Squirrel was frisking off, when Minnie called, "Wait, wait! Couldn't you—"

"O, you mustn't ask any favors. I'm full of business and care. Since we parted I have found a mate; and have a nest of my own, and lots of little ones. Call and see us!"

He had hardly gone, when Mrs. Yellow-bird came in sight. "My dear friend," Minnie began.

"A pretty friend!" she interrupted; "think of the trouble you've caused me!"

"How?"

"Ah, you can pretend not to know; but I am sure Master Squirrel has told you what he did, in spite, because I helped carry the humming-bird home for you, one day, and tipped him out of the car. You never even came to say you were sorry."

"How could I? I do not even know what the mischief was."

"He upset my nest, and killed all my pretty little birds!" And she poured forth a song that seemed to say, "All my little ones, all my pretty birds gone! I can never be happy again!"

Even after yellow-bird was out of sight, the sad notes of her song came back, and she never knew of the tears that Minnie shed for her.

A spider now let herself down by her silken thread from the bough above, where she had been listening to Minnie's words, and pitying her sorrow.

"Come! this is no way to be happy," she said, "and no way to make friends. Who'd care to know such a ragged little witch as you? And you're dusty as a toad. Why don't you wash your face, and mend your gown, and let folks see you are good for something?"

"O, I have tried!" said Minnie, mournfully. "I tried to sew a new gown out of elm leaves; but they were so tender they wilted and tore before I could put them together. Then I picked some beautiful oak leaves, and they were so tough they blunted my needle, and frayed the spider-webs I was sewing with."

"O, well, come down in the grass, and see what we can do together."

Down leaped Minnie, like a squirrel, and down dropped spider on her silken thread. They ran through the grass together till they came to a dwarf-oak, from which Minnie picked the large leaves, while spider wove them together with her curious web.

Minnie seated herself on a mushroom, and watched her good-natured friend at work. Spider wove her threads back and forth, till the seams appeared to be laced together with silvery, silken cords. She finished each with silver tassels; and, when Minnie had dressed in her handsome gown, wove a scarf of silver-gauze to throw across her shoulders.

Then Minnie twisted grass-blades together, as yellow-bird had taught her, and made a strong girdle for her waist, and tucked a rose leaf under it for apron, and picked for bonnet a purple snap dragon, with a golden frill inside.

But, alas, the happy, laughing look was gone from Minnie's eyes; and the rags and the little sun-burnt face looked out beneath all her finery!

CHAPTER XXX.

STORK.

A few days after Minnie's escape from the pitcher-plant she heard the minnows telling each other about a dreadful creature, that had been wading in the brook, catching the fish in his wide bill, and gobbling them down two or three at a time.

She thought it must be the stork, and that she would keep out of his way; but, when he really came at last, she couldn't help feeling how nice it would be to sit high and dry on his back while he waded up and down the stream. So Minnie came out of her hiding-place, and asked stork if he remembered her.

"Don't I? It's all I have lingered here for—the hope of seeing my queer little woman again. My own home is far off, beside the blue ocean, where I can hear the pleasant music of the waves."

"How I should like to hear them!" Minnie exclaimed. "Do they make as loud a sound as the water of the brook?"

"Not much louder when the weather is fair; but, in a storm, they roar like thunder, and don't they throw dainty breakfasts upon the rocks for me, then!"

"What! honey, and rose leaves, and berries?"

"No; where should they come from? The waves bring good fat fish, and clams, and black lobster-claws, that get broken in the storm."

"O, dear, is that all?"

"If you like it better, they bring shells, and pebbles white as eggs, and beautiful seaweeds gay as any garden-flower, and little red crabs, and curious star-fish. Come home with me, and I'll show what the waves can do!"

MINNIE'S RIDE.

Minnie was not sorry to leave the brook, which had become so unsafe for her; and, besides, you know she was always ready for a change. So, begging the stork to bend his neck as near the ground as he could, she clambered upon his back. Then stork outspread his broad, strong wings, and up they flew, and on, on, on, I cannot tell how many miles, till they reached the ocean-side.

Minnie had seen wide rivers and lakes before; but never anything equal to this mighty ocean, which lay beneath them like an enormous mirror, as they flew, —like a great glittering floor of glass.

On one side it stretched far out—nothing but water—till it reached the sky; on the other, it was bordered by a beach of smooth, white sand, over which lay strewn the gay seaweeds, and pebbles, and shells, about which stork had told her.

Glad to stand on her feet again, Minnie skipped along the shore, stooping often to admire some smooth, pearly shell, or glistening pebble, or heap of shining bubbles thrown up by the waves, and changing like opals in the sun.

69

It seemed as if the little waves were chasing her; as if they ran up the smooth sand on purpose to kiss her feet; as if they were asking her to accept the pretty weeds and stones which they kept tossing on the beach.

"O, stork, what a beautiful place it is! We will stay here as long as we live!" she said.

"I don't know about that. The beach is a good place after a storm; but we can't dine on bubbles and pebbles, Minnie, so climb my back again, and I'll take you across to the rocks."

A long, black ledge, against which the waves kept dashing, to turn white with foam, and leap glittering into the air,—this was the place toward which stork now steered.

The little woman could not but tremble as she looked down upon all the restless waves which stretched on every side as far as she could see. It was a beautiful sight; but Minnie knew that, if she should fall, the ocean would swallow her more easily than ever stork swallowed a minnow in the brook.

The rocks were wet, they found, and slippery; half covered with coarse seaweed, that was brown as leaves in winter, and did not look like any growing thing. But, selecting a higher ledge, which the sun had dried, stork asked Minnie to sit here and rest, while he went in search of food.

At first she watched the beautiful glittering foam, which leaped so lightly into the air, and then rolled back from the stones, in scattered drops, like showers of red pearls.

Then a croak called Minnie's attention; and, looking across the rocks, she saw stork almost choking himself with trying to swallow a fish too large for his throat. Down it went, at last; and now she watched how cautiously and silently stork crept from stone to stone, lifting his wings that he might easier walk on tip-toe with his clumsy feet. Suddenly down went his snaky neck, and, when it rose, another fish was writhing in his bill.

The little girl was so absorbed in watching her friend at his work, that she did not notice how night was falling, until a gust of cold sea-air made a chill creep over her.

Then, looking about, she found that the water had risen on every side, so as almost to cover the rocks on which she sat. Stars one by one were coming out in the sky, and she called loudly for stork to take her back to the shore.

CHAPTER XXXI.

THE SEA-SHORE.

Minnie did not call the stork a minute too soon. He had just caught sight of his mate, and, rather stupid with eating so hearty a supper, was about to fly away, forgetting his new friend.

He did not tell her this, but treated her more kindly, perhaps, when he thought how near she came to being drowned by his neglect. For the tide, which rose every minute, would soon have swept her away.

What should he find for Minnie's supper? She was not partial to raw fish. It was too dark now to look for checkerberries and violet buds. Ah! he would find some snails, and she should pick them out from their pretty white shells. They were sweet as smelts, he told her.

But, when Minnie came to look at them, it seemed to her like eating worms, or bugs; and, though stork assured her that in England he had seen some of the finest people eat these snails, she could not make up her mind to put one in her mouth.

So, a bright thought struck stork. Leaving Minnie on the beach, he seized a clam, rose high in the air, and let it fall with such force that the shell broke; out dropped its contents, and the little girl was hungry enough to eat them with a relish.

And, on their way home, stork stopped where there were birds' eggs in plenty. Minnie remembered yellow-bird's grief over the loss of his young, and could not bear to rob the nests at first. But hunger drove her to it afterwards.

Stork settled into his own quiet nest at last, and Minnie, creeping under his wing to keep warm, slept soundly, lulled by the music of the waves.

The next morning Minnie found the beach all over star-shaped tracks, too small for the stork's great feet. She found, soon, that these belonged to a curious little bird, that came in flocks. These skipped about the beach, as if they were trying to dance, or learning to take their steps. They were not larger than a robin, but had long legs and bills, so as to wade and catch fish among the waves.

Minnie made friends with them, and offered to give them lessons in dancing, of which they seemed so fond; but they told her they had only learned their droll steps from a habit of skipping away from waves when the tide was coming in.

71

Still, they allowed her to arrange them for a contra dance, and, though she had some trouble in persuading part to wait while the others went through their figure, Minnie laughed till she was tired, with the funny sight they made.

As the tide left the beach, Minnie found plenty of rocks, and all along the crevices of the rock were snails, such as stork had brought her the night before; and, on the sides, barnacles, a kind of fish that, except it is white and hard, looks like some plant growing. In hollows, where there were pools of water, she saw purple mussels, their shells half open that they might enjoy the sun.

Then the seaweeds were different from anything she had ever seen. They were shaped like trees,—apple-trees, or willows, or elms; but were of the gayest colors you can think,—bright red, pink, purple, yellow, green, and some were jet black, and pretty shades of brown. Some had fruit on them,— dark yellow berries, or apples, with a rosy side like any on our trees, only small as the head of a pin. The tallest of the trees were not higher than the length of your hand. It was like a little fairy forest.

Then Minnie found, to her surprise, that the snails, which seemed so fastened into the rocks by their shell, moved, shell and all. She found them travelling in every direction,—but O, so slowly! It made her ache to see them. She could run across the beach a dozen times before a snail had moved an inch.

Sometimes she took them in her hands and carried them to the pool they were trying to reach; but they always said it made them dizzy and confused to fly along so fast, and they preferred their own slow way.

Sometimes the snails ran races with each other. That was a droll thing to watch, for they all travelled as slowly, it seemed to Minnie, as the minute-hand on the clock in her father's office. They would start together, large snails and little ones, white snails and yellow, brown and black, striped, spotted, shaded, dragging their houses after them. There was a pretty little fellow, with a shell so bright it looked like gold; he almost always won the race.

One day Minnie picked up a beautiful purple mussel-shell, lined with pearl, and with a ledge of pearl inside, that served her for a seat. She launched this on the waves, and they bore her out to sea, where she drifted on without a fear, she knew how to swim so well, in case her boat upset; and then the beach birds were always ready to sail alongside of her little bark, and they could carry tidings home, should any harm befall her.

CHAPTER XXXII.

STORM AND CALM.

Minnie was very happy at the shore. A stranger stork did come one day, and, mistaking her for a fish, suddenly snatch her from her boat; but she held his bill so fast that he was glad to drop her on the beach. And at dark she was sorely afraid of the lobsters that crawled about the rocks, blindly stretching their black claws for food; but they had never harmed her yet, and, on the whole, the tiny woman thought she was having a beautiful time.

She loved to chase the little dimpling waves; she was never tired of watching the flash of sunlight on the water by day, and at evening the sweet path of moonlight, that stretched so far, seemed like a path to her home,—if only she dared to trust herself on the waves!

Then all the changing colors of the water, and the pretty wreaths of foam, delighted her. She built a house, for herself, of such white pebbles and shells that it looked like a little marble palace. And the tables and seats inside, and the bed, were all beautiful mother-of-pearl.

But a storm came one day, and washed away her house, and dashed the waves so high upon the beach, that Minnie fled for her life.

It happened a spruce-tree stood not far from the shore; so she scrambled up into its branches, both to be sheltered from, and to watch, the storm.

It was awful to see the great waves rise and beat against the beach, as if they meant to wash the whole world away, and to hear the grating of the stones they clashed together, and see the great mats of seaweed they tore from the rocks, and the shells they swept out of their crevices, and tossed on the shore in heaps.

MINNIE AT HOME.

And the water kept rising, and rising, till it covered the beach, and came nearer and nearer, until it reached the roots of the very tree into which Minnie had climbed. It had been hard enough to bear the beating of the branches in the wind, but now must she be drowned, so far from her home, and no one ever dream what had become of her?

Minnie screamed with fright, and then, through the storm, she seemed to hear a low song, such as her mother used to sing, and, instead of the rough spruce branches, it seemed as if her mother's arms were about her now.

She opened her eyes in wonder. Could it be that the soft hand she had missed so long was stroking her curls once more? that the dear voice she had never thought to hear again was singing soft lullabies over her? that Allie was looking in her face, and Frank was holding her pale hand in his?

Yes, and, stranger still, her mother and Franky declared that they had been with her all the while. On that first day of my story, when the squirrel came, —it seemed years ago to Minnie, now,—she had fallen from the fence, and

74

bruised her head, and had been sick with a fever ever since, and they thought she must have dreamed these marvellous things.

Certain it was that, when the little girl looked in the glass, she found herself large as ever, though pale and very thin. Her gown, too, was made of muslin, instead of forest leaves; and, instead of being perched on a pine-bough, here she stood in her own father's home!

And here she resolved to stay and be content. For, whether awake or in a fever-dream, Minnie had learned this, that, let it be large or small, there is, in all this great wide world, no place so safe and pleasant as our home. And this, besides, that the handsomest, kindest, gayest among strangers, will never make up for the loss of our own friends, the parents that have watched over us ever since we were born, the brothers and sisters that have played by the same fireside, and under the same green trees.

Dear children, when you are older, you will find that all the people in this world have strayed, like Minnie; that they wander about, making acquaintance with many creatures, but still unsatisfied; that they encounter storms, and suffer weariness and loneliness, and long for those who dwell in the far-off home.

Yes, and some morning we all shall wake in our Father's house, and find about us the blessed voices and dear forms of those we have loved; and then it will be like a dream that we seemed to lose them once.

That home is on the other side of the stars. But Frank and Minnie are young yet, and expect to find it here. They are young, and cannot believe that their senses may be mistaken, and that all Minnie's curious changes happened in a dream. Many an afternoon they still spend in looking for the wondrous weed that will make them understand the language of birds, and squirrels, and butterflies.

And, to tell you the truth, I more than half believe they will find it yet.